Royal House of Leone

TAMING
The ROYAL
BEAST

by Jennifer Lewis

1

Bella Beauvoir needed a boyfriend, and she needed one now.

She scanned the airport terminal, wondering which of these strangers would be least likely to knock her out cold if she flung her arms around him.

She flinched as her phone pinged again. She braced herself to open another text from the last man in the world she wanted to hear from.

I love you.

She was tempted to type something caustic in reply, perhaps **Is that what you tell your wife?** But she knew not to engage. With any luck he'd think she was already on her flight and would give up chasing her.

Her heart pounded and her nerves zinged with adrenaline. She was desperate to get on her plane before he found her and made a scene. She'd made it through security and to her gate, but that didn't mean she was home free. Her worst Tinder mistake was determined—or psychotic—enough to buy a plane ticket just to make a point.

I see you.

Her gaze darted back toward the security area where she'd seen the man that just last week she'd thought was nearly irresistible, retrieving his phone and watch from a tray.

She glanced around, and her eyes settled on a very tall, dark-haired man leaning against a broad column. He was engrossed in reading something on his phone and oblivious to his surroundings. His two-day stubble and faded jeans suggested an easygoing approach to life—and perhaps to strange damsels in distress.

From the corner of her eye she could already see Lucas Wall striding toward her, his pale eyes no doubt on fire with a mix of unspent desire and fury that she'd had the gall to reject him.

I'm meeting my boyfriend at JFK. Bella had texted him earlier in the midst of a volley of his texts about how he hated his wife and wanted to leave her and how she had to stay and give him a chance.

Ugh. She'd never have swiped right if she knew he was married. He'd taken her to Shakespeare in the Park and in a helicopter over Manhattan and charmed her with sushi and dry wit. He hadn't told her about his wife until the fourth date. Now he was obsessed with her and she couldn't stand the sight of him.

Her hackles rose as she felt Lucas closing in on her. She edged closer to the unknown man with the stubble. He—apparently riveted by whatever he was reading—didn't seem to notice her approach.

"Bella!" She cringed as Lucas's voice rang out.

It's now or never. She took one more step forward—a leap of faith, really—and flung her arms around the tall stranger.

Her face met his chest with a bump, smooshing her nose into the front of his pale blue shirt. He smelled of harsh deodorant soap—oddly reassuring. "Pretend you know me, please!" she hissed into his shirt front.

She felt his arms close around her, one hand still holding his phone. She looked up and for a split second she saw the mix of curiosity and alarm in his coffee-brown eyes before she craned herself up and kissed him on the mouth.

Her eyes closed automatically—who kissed with their eyes open?—and she pressed herself against him as if she might be able to disappear into him and escape this whole awkward scene. His lips were firm and soft at the same time, and his mouth parted slightly as if he was going to actually kiss her, even though she only needed it to look convincing.

She ignored an alarming surge of…something and strained for the sound of Lucas's voice.

Lucas wasn't calling her name. She pulled back enough to look up at her victim and say, "I've missed you so much!" as loudly as she dared.

He hesitated for a moment, expression blank, then blinked. "I don't know how I've managed to get along without you." His deep voice boomed impressively.

Relief rushed through her. "I wasn't sure you were going to make the flight." She attempted to think of what a normal couple might say.

"You thought I'd miss my trip to Zurich with you?" He played along, a smile dancing at one corner of his broad mouth.

"I can't wait to get away. I wish they'd start boarding." Bella glanced at the counter, arms still firm around his waist. Now that she dared to catch her breath she noticed how hard and athletic his body was beneath the casual clothing.

In answer to her prayers, they called for first-class passengers on her flight.

"That's us."

She gulped. "I don't have a first-class ticket."

"Don't worry. Come with me."

Neither of them had a big bag—she just had her purse and he had a battered leather briefcase—as they strode toward the desk together. In a rash moment she glanced back and saw Lucas, standing, feet apart and arms dangling, staring at her with a mix of shock and annoyance on his too-handsome face.

She ignored him.

The stranger counted out hundred dollar bills, upgrading her ticket before she could launch an effective protest. As they walked down the narrow corridor onto the plane she insisted that she'd pay him back as soon as they landed, silently wondering if she had enough in her account for that.

Probably not.

"Would you like the window?" He asked as if they'd known each other for ages.

The wide first-class seats looked so comfortable after her frantic morning of packing and running to catch the first flight she could get out of New York. "Oh, I don't care. Whichever you want."

He ushered her in. "I like to stretch my legs in the aisle."

She couldn't help glancing down at his legs, broad thighs encased in pale denim. "They are pretty long." She grinned, then immediately wished she'd kept her mouth shut. She'd already kissed this poor man and spent his money. Now she was going to leer at him?

They settled themselves into their seats. "I suppose I should ask what that was about."

Bella kept one eye on the door, where passengers eased in and down the aisle. Had Lucas actually boarded the plane? If she'd managed to upgrade to first at the last minute, there must be open seats. What on earth would she do if he followed her all the way to Zurich?

"I went on a couple of dates with him then he told me he's married." The words stuck in her throat. "I said I wouldn't see him again, and he freaked out and started following me around." She closed her eyes for a moment, letting the guilt wash over her. "I told my dad and he said I should come home."

"Where's that?"

"Altaleone. It's a small country between—"

"I know where it is." His dark eyes regarded her with amusement.

"You've been there?"

"Once or twice."

"I was born there but I haven't actually lived there since I was eight. My mom died and I was sent away to boarding school and since then I've kind of been on the road ever since. I visit my dad for Christmas but this is the first time he's asked me to come home." She paused to catch her breath. "Sorry, I'm rambling."

"Indeed you are."

"Do you live in New York."

"I do."

Not the chatty sort, was he? She probably should just leave him in peace now that he'd rescued her. Still… "What do you do?"

"I'm a lawyer."

"Oh." Yikes. Lawyers were trouble. "I worked for a law firm in the city." Her friend Melissa was a paralegal there and had got her the interview. "I don't think they'll be sad to see the back of me. I really want to work with animals. For the last few months I volunteered in a shelter on weekends and that was way more satisfying than my real job. But my landlord wouldn't even let me adopt a cat."

"Hmmm."

"I'm going to get a cat once I get home. And a dog. And anything else that needs rescuing." A smile spread across her face at the thought. Her dad had said she could stay with him and that he wouldn't mind an animal or two. His house was huge, with bedrooms to spare. And she'd finally have time to get to know him. Sometimes it felt like they were barely more than strangers. Her chest filled with emotion at the thought of actually living with him, and sharing dinner with him every night. Bella felt like her whole life was starting over.

The usual announcements were made and the plane started to taxi. Phew. She'd made her escape.

"Thanks again for rescuing me."

"You're welcome."

Her other conversational gambits went no further. Not a people person, clearly. Shame, since he was a great kisser.

Three weeks later

"Romance is the last thing I need." Rigo growled at his brother Sandro. "And if you insist on trying to shove women down my throat I'll get on the next plane back to New York." Rigo sat at the desk in his father's old study at the palace. Decades of piled paperwork obscured the polished walnut. And people kept bothering him with trivialities.

"I'm just saying that love is in the air right now, and with my wedding coming up I want everyone to be as happy as I am."

"Well, take your happiness and stick it where the sun don't shine because I have work to do."

The door to the study swung open, and his sister Beatriz poked her head in. "I just interviewed the latest candidate, and she seems perfect."

"Is she pretty?" asked Sandro, glancing at Rigo with mischief in his eyes.

"Shut up, Sandro," said Beatriz. "She's intelligent, seems reasonably capable and cloyingly sweet. A perfect lady-in-waiting."

Rigo snorted. "Do we have to use that stupid title when we're really looking for an administrative assistant?"

"It's tradition," said Beatriz wryly.

Rigo cursed under his breath. Tradition and all its nonsense rituals were half the reason he'd decamped to New York at the earliest opportunity. "Let me guess, her blue blood and winning smile are her most important qualifications."

Beatriz shrugged. "She fits the bill, that's all. I couldn't not interview her. Her father is a local bigwig."

"Great, hiring by nepotism." Rigo sighed. "Just what we need."

"Give her the benefit of the doubt, Rigo," said Beatriz. "She's in the dining room. Shall I send her in?"

"Sure. These piles of papers should scare her off." She probably thought it would be all garden parties and charity balls.

Beatriz smiled. "Great. I'll go get her."

Sandro followed Beatriz out, leaving Rigo alone and annoyed that yet another palace obligation was distracting him from the investigation into who killed his father and grandmother.

A knock on the door drew his grudging, "Come in."

The door opened and a petite girl in a white, lacy dress came in. Recognition crashed through him like a thunderbolt. The girl from the airport.

"Hello, I'm Bella Beauvoir." Panic flashed in her eyes as she thrust out her hand.

"I know. I believe we've had the pleasure of kissing."

Her face flushed. "I'm sorry, your majesty. It was an emergency."

"For God's sake don't ever call me that again." He sighed and glanced at her ruffled dress. "Are you on your way to your own wedding?"

"What?" Confusion clouded her hazel eyes.

He gestured to the garment, which almost reached the floor.

"Oh!" A grin spread across her annoyingly pert features. "It actually was my mom's wedding dress. I found it in a chest and decided to upcycle it. The lace is handmade, and it seemed a shame for it to sit in a box. I cut out all the petticoats and shortened the hem."

"How riveting." He felt his eyes narrow. Long, dark ringlets cascaded over her shoulders in a most unprofessional manner. She'd never have made it past the HR department in New York. "Do you realize I'm looking for a secretary to organize and catalog all this paperwork?" He gestured at the teetering piles of yellowed pages and dog-eared manila folders.

"They did explain that to me just now." She smiled wanly. "I love organizing things."

He snorted. "Really." Typical vapid, pretty aristocrat's daughter. He hated the type. "And why do you want this job?"

"I'm looking for a challenging and interesting position." A bright smile.

He lifted a brow.

Her expression faltered. "There aren't a whole lot of jobs here in Altaleone. I'm planning to start a small animal sanctuary so I need to work locally so I can be there when the animals need me."

Rigo suppressed a deep groan. But if he didn't hire her there might be an endless stream of unsuitable candidates wasting his time and the work was hardly challenging. He decided to trust his sister Beatriz who knew more about palace life than he did. "When can you start?"

Her face brightened. "I could start right now."

"Tomorrow will be fine. Be here at eight."

She blinked. "That's very early."

"If you're not interested I—"

"I'll be here," she interrupted. Then she leaned over the desk and thrust out her hand. "Thank you for the opportunity."

"See you in here tomorrow at eight. I'll tell security to expect you." He stood and took her hand with reluctance. It was soft and small, but her handshake was reasonably firm. Bella Beauvoir had no doubt drifted through life by being rich and noble and pretty, and it irked him that she was going to sail right into a prestigious palace job the same way. Still, he'd only keep her as long as she was useful to the investigation.

2

Bella walked home to her new ground floor flat in Casteleone. Her father would be thrilled that she got the job. He'd been hammering on about it since the moment she got off the plane and it had taken forever to finally get the interview.

She was a little sad that he'd shunted her into town so quickly, but he was right about his house being a bit too far out of the way, and he hadn't been too pleased when she came home from her first trip into town with two different stray dogs. The next day word had got around and she acquired a neurotic black and white ferret and a rather vocal scarlet macaw. On day three she came home with a beautiful rat and her father told her to find a new residence.

She couldn't wish for an easier commute. Her rooms were on the first floor of an old house that she loved for its small garden, with a brick wall high enough to keep her new pets safe. She hadn't been entirely forthcoming on her application about her pets. She'd mentioned that she had a dog. Which was true.

Ari, the fluffy golden cat with blue eyes who'd been living there when she moved in, rubbed himself around her legs as she closed the gate behind her. Tintin, the fluffy white terrier, rushed up, barking, with Suki the sausage dog hot on his heels.

"Hello, my lovelies! Things are looking up for us. Dad will be happy, and I'll earn the money to buy us all a nice home." Since her dad was wealthy people often expected her to have money herself, a fat trust fund or inheritance from an aged aunt, but she didn't. So far she'd managed to survive thanks to an expensive education and a network of kind friends moving into increasingly high places and helping her land jobs there. But it was time to strike out on her own and do what she was meant to do.

She could hear Pepe the scarlet macaw screeching impatiently from the bedroom, and it made her smile. "Coming! Keep your feathers on!" He'd been shut in a back room by his former owner, who couldn't stand his loud cries, and he'd become so stressed out that he'd started plucking all his feathers out. "Hello, beautiful." She opened the cage door and let him hop onto her hand. She stroked his thin feathers, and he cocked his head to the side and watched her. "Was everyone good today?"

He responded with a raucous cry.

"Really?" She looked at Suki. "Is he fibbing?"

Suki shook herself, her big ears flying.

"See, Pepe? She says she was good."

Her phone rang, and she put Pepe gently down on the back of the sofa. Her heart soared when she saw who it was. "Hi, Dad."

"Sweetheart." His deep voice always sent a wave

of emotion through her. Possibly because she didn't hear it all that often. "Did you go to the palace like I asked?"

"Yes." She leaned down and stroked Ari, who writhed between her legs. "I was interviewed by five different people."

"Did you dress appropriately?"

"I wore my prettiest dress."

"Good. And you made sure they knew who you are?"

"I didn't have to. I think they knew everything about me. I was at day school in the village with half of the Leone kids anyway." She loved that the royal family sent their children to the local school. At least until they were old enough to be packed off to respectable boarding schools like she was. "I got the job."

"Excellent. Your mother would be so proud of you."

Would she? Her mom had been gone so long now she could barely remember her face or the sound of her voice. "Thanks. I hope I won't screw it up. I'm not all that great in an office."

"You'll do fine, just smile and be nice to everyone."

"I think I can pull that off." She'd learned that she tended to do best in jobs like retail and customer service rather than the prestigious jobs her father would admire. She had a gift with animals, but her science grades weren't good enough to pursue veterinary studies so her employment history was checkered at best. At least now he'd be proud she was at the palace.

"It's only a ten-minute walk from my house so

it should work out really well."

"Excellent. And don't forget to update me daily with what you're working on."

"Apparently they're going to have me going through a lot of papers."

"What kind of papers?"

"I have no idea. But why would you care?" Her dad had been friends with Prince Emil and had hunted with him regularly, but after his death he hadn't been near the place except for King Darias's coronation, which had been attended by almost everyone in the country.

"They're still casting around looking for whoever murdered the queen and her son." She heard the flick of the lighter for one of his cigars. "I want to help the investigation however I can."

"Of course. I'll keep you posted." Tintin jumped up on her and landed his fluffy white paws near her knees. She laughed at his serious expression.

"What's so funny?"

"Little Tintin. If he were a bigger dog he'd have knocked me right—"

"Got to go. Call me after your first day." He hung up before she could finish her sentence. Her dad was always busy and in the middle of something, though she didn't have much of a clue what he did all day.

Maybe telling him about her job would bring them closer together. It was refreshing to have him show an interest in her activities. She picked up Tintin and kissed him on the nose. "I'll do my best to make him proud." Tintin licked her face enthusiastically.

Early the next morning, Rigo summoned Gibran into his office—his dad's study—and asked him to sit down. "As you pointed out to me, Ms. Beauvoir's father is a member of the infamous Cross of Blood. Beatriz is convinced she'll be good for the role but I want to keep an eye on her in case she's been sent here as a mole, or even to disrupt our investigation."

Gibran nodded. "We must watch her carefully. I have a camera set up in here, also in the billiard room and the yellow dining room, all places she could set up and work. Let me know if you need cameras anywhere else."

"Give me a day or so to feel her out and figure out what I'm going to do with her. I love the idea of being able to watch her zero in on the useful material in the piles of papers we're drowning in." Rigo leaned forward and rested his elbows on the desk. "None of the family knows our suspicions about her?"

"No. As you suggested, the less they know, the safer they are. They're aware that we tried to call the Cross of Blood members in for questioning and that each of them was able to avoid the summons due to a legal technicality of one sort or another."

"Which only raises my suspicions. The main reason I flew here from New York is to comb through Altaleone law, going back to the Roman Empire if I have to, to find a way to subpoena them. I'm close. I found a good precedent in the 1600's when a group of aristocrats were accused of treason. Give me time and I'll find a way to get them all in here."

A knock on the door made them both turn. Gibran rose to his feet.

"Come in." Rigo shot Gibran a meaningful glance. If it was Bella she was fifteen minutes early, perhaps hoping to overhear something.

The door opened, and she entered with a smile on her face. Her long, dark curls still sprawled carelessly over her shoulders, and today's dress had large flowers and a lace petticoat. "Hello. I came early."

Rigo hated it when people stated the obvious. "This is Gibran Al Nazariyah, head of security at the Palace."

She thrust out a hand and shone her bright smile on Gibran, who returned his usual stony gaze along with a grudging handshake.

"Are you ready for me or should I come back in fifteen?" She looked cheerfully from one to the other.

"Gibran and I are finished talking. Today, I'd like you to organize some paperwork by date." Gibran slid out noiselessly. Rigo picked a big marbled cardboard filing box off the floor and heaved it onto the desk. "These are tax filings from the Altacord Trading Group, from the 1950s and '60s. I had the revenue service pull them, but they're jumbled in the box without rhyme or reason. I'd like you to arrange them with the most recent in the front, and also create a database file with the amount of gross earnings declared, the net earnings declared, and the amount of taxes paid in each calendar year."

He watched her face closely, looking for signs

of interest. Her father was a principal partner in Altacord, which was the second-largest diamond broker in Altaleone, a position he'd inherited from his father and grandfather and great-grandfather— going back many generations.

She looked mildly horrified, which sent a teeny ripple of excitement up his spine. "Is there a problem?"

"Um, the database software. Is it Excel?"

Rigo stared. Was she too incompetent even to do such a simple task? "I'd imagine so." He handed her a small laptop that had been stripped back to the operating system and basic software. "I'm sure you'll figure it out." Worst-case scenario he'd have someone redo the work if these files were of real interest, which he doubted. His goal today was to watch her and get a bead on both her goals and her competencies.

She picked up the laptop, opened it, and pressed the power button. She frowned slightly while it loaded.

"You look nervous." He wanted to see how she'd react.

She looked up fast, big eyes wide. "Oh, no." That quick, flashy smile again, pearly white teeth that were no doubt the result of expensive orthodontistry. Then she turned her attention back to the laptop and licked her lips. The sight of her pink tongue flashing out of her soft mouth sent of bolt of utterly inappropriate heat to his groin, and he tugged his gaze to the wood trim near the ceiling.

She was toying with him. And he was weak enough to respond. "Let me carry the box of files to the billiard room for you," he said gruffly. He wanted her out of there.

"Oh, I'm sorry! I'm in your way." She rose to her feet in a flurry of loose curls and lace petticoats. "I can carry it."

"That's okay." He wanted to make sure she didn't wander off course and end up somewhere outside the view of their high-powered cameras and sound-recording devices. "I've got it." He heaved the file box into his arms.

Bella brought the still-open laptop, as well as her leather satchel. As she stood up he could swear he heard a squeaky noise.

He waited while she exited the door ahead of him and heard it again, followed by a strangled cry for help that tore at his nerves. "What was that?"

"I didn't hear anything." She turned that pearly smile on him again.

As they walked through the door a high-pitched screech made his hair stand on end. She simply tossed her hair and marched ahead.

"Ms. Beauvoir. I believe something is trapped in your bag and screaming to be let out."

3

Bella walked along the corridor without looking back. Her long floral skirt swished about her legs. "Oh, that's my ferret, Squiggles. He won't be any trouble, I promise. He gets upset if I'm away from him too long, but he'll be quite happy in my bag all day."

Rigo stared, speechless for a moment. "He doesn't sound happy."

"He doesn't much like moving. He's more of a staying-in-one-place ferret."

"In here to the right." Rigo refused to be sidetracked by a ferret. "You can sit at this table." He knew where the hidden cameras could get the best view. "And spread the papers out while you get them in order."

"Great." She turned, curls flying, and shone her pearly smile on him. "I'll be as quick as I can."

"Accuracy is more important than speed," he said sternly. "And I'd like you to take a look at each tax return and make notes about it in the database. Add a longer column to the far right for that." He'd improvised this last instruction to gauge both her level of interest in her father's affairs and her own intelligence—or lack thereof.

"Sure." She pulled out the chair, set her bag carefully on the table in front of her, and pushed up the lace-trimmed cuffs of her dress.

"Is there anything else you need?"

"A cup of tea would be lovely." She said it innocently. Then laughed. "But you're a prince so you don't get tea. Is there somewhere I can make myself some?"

Rigo stared at her for a moment. "No."

"Oh. Okay then." Her smiled faltered. Good. "I'll get down to work."

Rigo turned and left, fighting the urge to roll his eyes. Her behavior in the airport showed that she was used to using men to fill her needs with no thought for their feelings. Just because she had big eyes with long eyelashes and a curvy body beneath all the roses and petticoats, she thought she could wrap him around her little finger.

She couldn't be more wrong.

"That was a close one, Squiggles. Didn't I tell you to be quiet?" Bella unlatched the satchel and let him poke his inquisitive nose out. "Not everyone appreciates having a member of the mustelid family in their home. Now don't distract me, or I'll forget what I'm supposed to be doing." The lady who'd rescued Squiggles told her his hair had only just grown back after all falling out due to stress when his owner died. She didn't want to risk a recurrence.

She opened the laptop, mildly curious to see what was on a royal laptop—did it have the family crest as a screensaver? All she found was the basic software package, which included—thank heaven—the same version of Excel she'd had the misery of using to catalog expenses at the law firm.

She'd created the basic table and headers when she noticed Rigo standing in the doorway again. He was very tall, with a countenance as chiseled as the mountain peaks of his ancestral homeland. His brown eyes smoldered with an intimidating intelligence, and she was sure he could see right through her. It was awkward that she'd kissed him. Yes, it had been an emergency and had saved her a lot of drama, but she wished she didn't remember how soft and warm his mouth felt under hers or what taut muscles he had.

Why wasn't he saying anything? He stood there, watching her. Her attempt at a friendly smile froze on her lips, and she fixed her eyes on her database program. "Does this look right?"

He frowned and walked slowly over, then leaned to look at her screen—he smelled like the mountains on an icy winter morning—and she felt her heart beat faster. Probably sheer terror.

His eyes narrowed for an instant, causing her gut to clench. "Looks fine. Then he turned and swept out the door.

She collapsed into her chair and heaved a sigh.

Goodness, he made her tense! Rigo Leone was worse than all the stuffed shirts at the law firm put together. She'd have to do an amazing job so she didn't get fired and lose this opportunity to earn money and make her dad happy.

Though she still didn't understand why her dad was so keen for her to work there. Bragging rights, maybe. "My daughter's at the palace." She could here him murmuring the news to his friends through a cloud of cigar smoke. Maybe he saw her as a way to maintain his royal connections.

Maybe he wants me to marry one of the Leone brothers.

The thought occurred to her with thunderclap suddenness.

Not Rigo, though. Definitely not Rigo. And Darias and Sandro were already spoken for. None of the others even lived in Altaleone, as far as she knew.

Sorry, Dad.

She'd count this whole adventure a success if she could stay there six months without getting fired. That would beat her two and a half months before the final straw at the Paris PR firm—she'd spilled wine on an important client—and nearly five months at the Zurich law firm before the baby rat she was fostering had escaped from her backpack, chewed through the top layer of meeting minutes, and drawn some blood-curdling screams from the head admin.

She pulled the first file from the pile and suppressed a groan. Tax returns from 1964. *Focus. You can do it.*

"Do you think her father sent her here to spy on us?" Gibran was back in Rigo's office. He'd called him as soon as they'd picked it up on the mic and—now that she'd left for the day—had just played it for him.

"I suspect so but I'm not sure she knows it." Rigo knew that the staff was under heavy surveillance after at least one member had proven to be an enemy in their midst. "He may have something specific in mind that he wants her to accomplish. I want to figure out what that is." He shoved a hand through his hair. "Maybe she'll tell her ferret about it."

Gibran didn't smile. He reminded Rigo of his favorite prosecutor in New York. The one who never let go, who kept turning up rocks and finding some new evidence to prevent a case from collapsing—tireless, unsmiling, and always successful in the end.

Rigo planned to spend the midnight oil going back through the tax returns Bella had studied that day and looking for anything she'd missed or deliberately ignored or misrepresented in her database.

He looked up at Gibran, who sometimes appeared to have superhuman patience. "I know you've been frustrated by your inability to nail down the murderers, but it's obvious from events of the last year that the motivations of the family's enemies are largely financial, or related to feeling cheated out of an inheritance."

"Who's been cheated out of an inheritance?" His sister Beatriz opened the door and walked in.

"Your fiancé, for one," said Rigo drily. "Or so his family contends."

"If Lorenzo is still a suspect I'm going to throttle you with my bare hands."

"He fits the profile nicely—disgruntled aristocrat with an ancient ax to grind—but he made a smart move in proposing to you. It'll likely keep his head off the chopping block."

There was an actual chopping block in the courtyard of the old castle in Casteleone.

"Ha ha." Beatriz tilted her head. "I just saw

Bella Beauvoir walking out of here talking to her satchel. Doesn't seem like she's changed much since we were at school together. She was always a bit eccentric. I'm glad she took the job so Mama will have someone to help her while I'm busy in Milan." Beatriz had recently started a fashion line and would no longer have time for the kind of tiresome royal duties Rigo had always prided himself on avoiding.

"If she ever comes back." Their widowed mom had surprised them all by meeting an old flame and marrying him suddenly in Paris.

"She'll be back next week, with Amadou. They're going to stay until after the wedding. She's especially excited to see you. She says she hasn't seen you in Altaleone for years apart from Papa's funeral."

Rigo stiffened as guilt and misgivings soaked through him. His last words with his father had been harsh ones and more than four years ago. Now they'd never have a chance to make up.

He'd hoped that Gibran would solve the mystery of the murder, and Rigo could keep himself buried in his important legal work in New York. He'd left several hot cases burning a hole in his desk, and while he trusted his associates, he didn't want to stay here one minute longer than he had to. For all its natural beauty Altaleone reminded him too much of things he wished he didn't know.

"Darias and Emma are coming for dinner. Lorenzo's here talking to Sandro and Serena in the living room."

"Isn't that festive," growled Rigo. "Don't you

people have work to do?"

"Even you have to break to eat, brother dearest." Beatriz left and closed the door behind her.

"Everything has to be a damn social occasion with this family. Would you care to join us?"

"No, thanks." Gibran's expression didn't move.

"A man after my own heart."

Rigo marched into dinner, determined to eat and run as fast as possible. Not that he didn't appreciate his family, but he needed to go through the paperwork Bella had organized today.

Sandro sat next to him and clapped him on the back. "Rigo, we need to find you a date for my wedding."

"Nonsense. We're watching a ceremony, not heading onto Noah's ark."

"There'll be dancing," explained Serena. "Sandro's friend Louis is coming from New Orleans to arrange the catering, and he's bringing a small jazz band."

"I don't dance." He took a swig of red wine.

"Everyone else will be paired off. Even Mama," protested Beatriz. "We'll find you a nice girl."

"What if I don't want a nice girl?"

"Then we'll find you a sexy man," said Sandro with a wink.

Rigo sighed. "I came here to solve a problem that apparently no one else can solve. If you don't like the way I'm doing it, I'll head back to my busy office in New York. I'm certainly not going to waste my time dancing and making small talk with some empty-headed heiress hell-bent on marrying a prince. Will dinner be served before I grow old and die?"

He glanced toward the kitchen hallway, where an alarmed-looking staffer hurried in with a big bowl of salad.

"Great. Rabbit food."

"There's potato and leek soup and a big poached bass," said Beatriz. "Besides, if you want something specific all you have to do is ask. There's no need to be so crabby."

Not Beatriz too? She was usually the most sensible of the bunch. Since she'd fallen head over heels for Lorenzo she was as bad as the rest of them. "I'm not crabby."

A snort of laughter from the left drew his attention, but since he wasn't sure who it came from he decided to ignore it.

"Come on, Rigo. You must have a girlfriend." Darias had finally showed up and taken a seat on the far side of the table. "I lived in New York too, remember. The most beautiful women in the world live there." He smiled at his wife, Emma, and Sandro's fiancée, Serena, both of whom had been independent, freewheeling New Yorkers until they had the misfortune to be swept into the royal Borg.

"My sex life is none of your concern." He ate a bite of crispy hamster chow.

"Who's talking about sex?" said Sandro. "It's your romantic life we're interested in."

"Why?" He scowled at his brother.

"Because you're working too hard and you don't come home enough. You need a sensible woman to get your life back in balance."

"This world isn't run by people with balanced lives." He put his fork down. "Can we focus on the issue at hand? The burning question of who murdered our father and grandmother?" Anything to get them out of his personal life. He stood and closed the two tall doors into the dining room, making sure the staffers were outside. "I need to interrogate the key players in the Cross of Blood society."

"Gibran has said we can't get near them. They're lawyered up and won't talk."

"And I think I know why. This organization has existed for hundreds of years—why?"

"It was formed to send troops to the Crusades. To defend Christendom from the infidel," said Darias drily.

"Do you really think the holy knights of Altaleone cared that much about what was going on in some distant so-called Holy Land a thousand miles away?"

"People's lives revolved around religion back then," said Emma.

"Or so they'd have you believe." Rigo leaned back. "The medieval church was an effective mechanism for the control and centralization of money and power. The confessional wasn't about expiating sin; it was about having the dirt on everyone in the parish. The Crusades weren't about religion but about riches."

"That's a very cynical view," said Darias.

"My time practicing law has given me a depressing amount of insight into human nature." Rigo walked around the table. "And from where I'm standing the Cross of Blood was formed so the locals could rape and pillage in foreign lands, bring the wealth back here without paying taxes on it, then grow and augment it over the centuries without the scrutiny of anyone but themselves."

"They all own legitimate businesses."

Rigo snorted. "They all own businesses. Do you really think a mountaintop vineyard can sustain a lavish lifestyle for centuries? In my opinion most of their businesses are nothing more than a front so no one looks for the source of their ill-gotten wealth."

Darias frowned. "There is that Swiss account. After Emma was kidnapped for the access code, I did some digging to find out how much was in it and was unable to find an answer. The code I have identified an account but didn't allow permission to view it or even see the balance. Since the account isn't in Altaleone I can't even go royal on them and demand access."

"Perhaps someone could hack into the computer," said Sandro.

"We don't want to commit a crime to solve a crime," muttered Rigo. "But I believe this account might be making distributions to the members."

"And who's running it?"

"That's what we need to find out. That may be the person who decided that our family members were disposable. Maybe Dad was asking too many questions. I don't see any record of taxes being paid on that money—ever."

"And in Altaleone there is an annual tax on investment gains," said Beatriz. "Regardless of where the money is held."

"Exactly." Darias frowned. "It's at the core of our ability to redistribute wealth among our population so everyone has a high living standard."

"I suspect the Cross of Blood cronies see themselves as living above or outside the laws of Altaleone and carrying on in their own manner as they have for centuries, keeping the wealth in their own coffers."

"But why would they want to kill?"

"Maybe Grandma or Papa threatened to expose them." Beatriz looked intrigued. "The loss of their main source of wealth would be a huge blow. They'd actually have to survive on the measly few millions that their vineyards and diamond-trading endeavors bring in. That's barely enough to redo the slate roof on a medieval castle."

"Beatriz would know. She just renovated her own place." Lorenzo smiled at her.

"You could be onto something." Darias sipped his wine slowly.

A knock on the door tightened Rigo's muscles. While he half wanted word of his theory to get out—crooks had a way of covering their tracks that only made them more obvious—he preferred to get further in his paper investigation before his suspicions spread outside the palace. "One moment," he called.

"So how do you plan to expose this activity?" whispered Beatriz.

"I'm starting with Maurice Beauvoir." Rigo mouthed the words in near silence. "I'm setting his daughter up to leave a trail of bread crumbs right into his finances, and wherever things don't add up, I'll pounce."

"Oh." Beatriz's face fell. "She seems so sweet."

"Not as sweet as you think." He was growing increasingly sure that her ditzy brunette facade was an act.

"What if you're wrong?" asked Darias.

"I'm never wrong."

4

Bella loved her short walking commute to the palace, and even Squiggles barely complained. She sailed past security and was seated at the dining room table—it was a second dining room that no one used—and going through the tedious paperwork five minutes before she was even supposed to be here.

Someone had moved her files around. Maybe the cleaning staff. She shrugged and pulled open a tax return from 1968. Mostly she was surprised by how little money the company made. Wasn't the 1960s the era when everyone wanted a big rock on their finger? But of course money was worth more then. Inflation and all that jazz.

She had just entered the taxes paid in her database when she realized that Rigo was leaning against the doorframe, watching her.

Why does it feel like he can read my thoughts? He's a lawyer, not a psychic. The way he looked at her made her feel like a criminal in the dock. Worse yet, it sent a totally inappropriate surge of heat to her core. What was that about? "Good morning."

"Is it?"

"Sorry. I didn't mean to be insincere or flippant

or…" *Polite.*

"Do you feel there's a conflict of interest in you looking through the files for Altacord Trading Group?"

"No. Why?"

"Because your father is a principal in it."

"Really? I haven't seen his name on anything."

"I believe he's what's known as a silent partner."

She frowned. "Someone who puts up money but doesn't participate in the day-to-day activities?"

"More or less."

"I had no idea." Her father never talked business to her. "But why would it be a conflict of interest?"

"If your father had…something to hide."

"Like what?" She didn't follow his train of thought. She heard a muffled rustling sound, then suddenly Rigo doubled over and let out a blistering curse.

Bella sprang to her feet. "Are you okay?" Was he having a heart attack?

"Your—" He cursed again. "Your vermin bit me on the ankle."

"Squiggles!" She dived around the table, scooped Squiggles up in her arms, and stroked his head. "You were just trying to help, weren't you?"

"Help?" Rigo spluttered. "How?"

"Perhaps he thought you were impugning my family honor." You had to see the humor in the situation.

Rigo's mouth didn't move a millimeter. He wasn't one to waste smiles. "Does your father know you're here?"

"Of course. He's very proud of me. Working in the palace is a dream job." She managed a cheery smile. "It really is. I can walk to work in less than ten minutes."

"I bet Squiggles appreciates the short commute." He spoke through gritted teeth.

Her heart sank. "Did he really bite you hard? Let me see."

"It's nothing." He didn't budge, so she retreated. "But I'd appreciate your making sure it doesn't happen again."

She inhaled sharply. "I'll leave him at home. He'll be fine in a box with a blanket over it. Sure, maybe all his hair will fall out again due to stress, but we'll—"

His brows lowered. "Have you found anything of interest in the files?"

"Only that the earnings for Altacord aren't that high. But I suppose that's business in a tiny country. And it's not a big company."

"What do you mean, not high?"

She propped Squiggles on one arm and reached for the 1968 file. "Profits in 1968 were only eight hundred and sixty seven thousand florins. It's before we switched to euros, but I think that's only about five hundred thousand euros in today's currency. I suppose I thought it would be millions."

Rigo took the file from her and flipped through it. "The gross profit isn't high either." He flipped through to the end in silence. "It's a small company. It will be interesting to see how profits grew over time."

"Yes." Her dad spent five million last year on a

yacht he kept in Montpelier, France, and used for a few weeks in the summer. "I suppose things were quieter back then."

Another tall, dark-haired man whom Bella recognized from the press as Rigo's brother Sandro poked his head in. "Huge favor to ask, bro. Could we borrow your new lady-in-waiting to help go through the RSVPs for the wedding? It's all hands on deck. We need to confirm the final numbers today so Louis knows how much fresh crawfish to bring from New Orleans."

Bella stifled a laugh. "I'd be happy to help."

"That's great!" Sandro's glamorous fiancée, Serena, stood behind him. Bella had watched her video on how to apply eyebrow pencil and decided she didn't need great eyebrows that badly. Right now Serena wasn't even wearing eyebrow pencil. Ha.

"Bella is engaged in important and time-sensitive work," said Rigo grimly. "Surely there are other palace staff who could—"

"Believe me, we've got everyone on it already. We sent out over a thousand invitations, and we need to figure out exactly who's coming and find somewhere for them to stay."

"Good lord. Isn't the wedding next week?"

"The week after." Serena smiled. "Don't worry. We'll figure it out."

"I wonder how they'll feel about sleeping in a tent city in the palace courtyard?" Rigo lifted a brow.

"Hey, that's a great idea!" Sandro punched him in the shoulder. Could two brothers be any more different? "Can we borrow Bella to order the tents?"

"If you must." Rigo sighed. "But I want her back as soon as possible."

Bella was happy to get away from the tax returns, if only for an hour. She stuffed Squiggles back in the bag, buckled it shut, and put in on her shoulder.

"Was that an ermine?" asked Serena.

"He's a ferret. With a Dalmatian coat," she said proudly. Squiggles had unusual coloring and got attention wherever they went.

"He's adorable."

"Thanks." And thank goodness the rest of the family wasn't as miserable as Cruel Prince Rigo. "When's your wedding?"

"The fifteenth. It was pulled together very quickly because, as you can probably tell, I'm pregnant."

Bella glanced down at Serena's belly, which was only just starting to show, at least in the floaty top she wore. "I hadn't noticed until you mention it. When are you due?"

"Nine months from last Christmas," chimed in Sandro. He leaned in and kissed Serena softly on the cheek. It was true about pregnant women glowing. Either that or Serena's highlighter application was really subtle and effective. She suspected the former.

The gossip papers were full of articles about Serena's whirlwind Cinderella-style romance with Prince Sandro, though it seemed she was something of a media celebrity in her own right. "Congratulations. Do you know if it's a girl or a boy, or is it rude to ask that?"

Serena smiled. "I don't think it's rude. It's a boy." She rested a hand on the waistband of her black pants. "We only just found out. I wanted to know so we could give him a name."

A pretty blonde woman waved as they headed into a much grander dining room where papers were spread all over the surface of a vast table. "Hi, Bella, I'm Emma." Bella knew Emma was Darias's wife who married him right before he became king. She'd read a salacious story on one website that she'd married him for money to pay for her drug-addicted brother's rehab, but you couldn't believe what you read on the Internet.

"Nice to meet you." She took a seat in front of a pile of unopened envelopes. Her dad would love her sitting around a table with all these nice royals. Emma introduced her to the other people sitting at the table, all palace staff she hadn't met yet, opening the big envelopes and organizing them into yes and no piles.

An older woman named Effi, who managed palace events, was checking off the names in a database and handing them to Katerin, a brunette with a pixie cut who was stacking them in "bride's guest" and "groom's guest" piles, then Sandro and Serena took them and tried to fit each of them into a huge paper chart with table placements for the dinner after the ceremony. Beatriz, Rigo's sister, was trying to figure out where each of the guests would sleep.

"For some reason we didn't realize what a huge job this would be," said Serena. "We should have hired more people to help Effi organize everything, but we were traveling abroad. So it's all a bit last minute. We really don't have any idea where we're going to put all these people. We were expecting at least thirty percent to say no, but so far almost all of them are coming."

"Who'd want to miss it?" said Bella. "It sounds like a fabulous party." As she spoke the last part she wondered if she was talking out of turn and should just open envelopes and keep her mouth shut.

"We're certainly hoping it will be," said Sandro. "Even if we have to stack people like sardines somewhere."

"We booked all the hotels in town, and with those, the palace, the castle, my house, and the orangerie we should be able to sleep about three hundred," said Beatriz.

"Which is about how many were in town for my wedding to Darias."

"What about the hunting lodge on the far side of town?"

Beatriz grimaced. "No one's stepped in there since Dad died. It probably hasn't been slept in for years. He mostly used the grounds for the hunt to meet. I suppose we could check. It's officially Rigo's now. Dad left it to him in his will."

"Doesn't it have upwards of thirty bedrooms?"

"Maybe more. They used to invite people from all over Europe for hunting parties in the old days."

"Worth a look then," said Sandro. "Perhaps you should drive out there and eyeball it."

"Then how can I find rooms for all these guests? None of you know the rooms as well as I do. Maybe Bella could go take some photos of the lodge to give us an idea of whether we could whip it into shape in less than two weeks."

She sat up in her chair. "I'd be happy to." An old hunting lodge sounded fabulous.

"Perfect. Ask Rigo for the keys."

Her chest tightened. Asking Rigo for anything would probably get her scowled at. "Okay."

"And you have a phone that can take decent pictures?"

"Sure." She whipped it out to show them, without disturbing Squiggles since her phone was in the front pocket of her bag.

"Send them to me as you take them." She and Beatriz exchanged texts to save each others' numbers, and she hoisted her bag gently on her shoulder and headed back to Rigo's office.

She knocked, heart already thumping.

"What?" His gruff retort was anything but welcoming.

"Uh." She opened the door a crack. Rigo's piercing brown eyes seared a hole right through her. "Your family would like me to go to your hunting lodge to take pictures."

He looked at her with noncomprehension.

"The house left to you by your father." Must be nice to have an estate you'd forgotten about. "Beatriz thinks it might be a good place to put up wedding guests."

"And I care because…?"

"She says you have the key."

Rigo snorted. "Does she think I carry it around on my key chain? Ask the security staff to figure out how to get you in there. They're keeping an eye on all the crown properties."

She wanted to ask whom she should speak to, but there were easier ways to find that out than asking Rigo. "No problem."

An hour later a stone-faced young man had driven her into the foothills of the mountains east of Casteleone and was unlocking the large wood double doors of a looming stone edifice that seemed to have been inspired by Grimm fairy tales.

It had actual castellated battlements. "I wonder if they've ever poured boiling oil down on invaders from up there?"

"The large glass windows suggest a later period. Nineteenth century revivalism, perhaps." The security guard made Rigo seem jovial.

"Oh." She stepped inside, camera at the ready. "Do you suppose there's electricity or will we have to light candles?"

The guard switched on a long bank of dated-looking switches, illuminating a series of black iron chandeliers and wall sconces. She switched on the flash in her phone and took some photos. The stone floor was laid in a pattern weaving light with dark stone. Dark wood paneling made the walls hard to capture, but the deep coffered ceiling had gold accents that caught the light.

The space had an austere beauty but could hardly be called comfortable. And there was barely any furniture. Just a grouping of two high-backed chairs near the vast carved stone fireplace, and in another room, a long, rectangular dining table with a scarred surface. The dining table had no chairs.

Upstairs, only one of the thirty-eight bedrooms had a bed in it, and that smelled very musty. The bathrooms looked to be of 1950s vintage, with heavy, white fixtures, and the whole place needed a good scrubbing.

She took a lot of photos and texted them to Beatriz, who occasionally asked her for a close up of something. Beatriz wanted more pictures of the grounds so she went outside to take them, the dour blond guard close behind her.

There was a walled enclosure that was probably once a vegetable or flower garden but now nothing grew there but unmowed grass dotted with wildflowers. What a perfect place for dogs to play! There was an old greenhouse whose glass had mostly fallen out of the frame and lay in smashed neglect on the ground, but the elaborate domed frame made her think what an amazing aviary it would make if you replaced the glass with netting.

The lawn around the castle—they could call it a lodge all they wanted, but she knew a castle when she saw one—had reverted to a soft meadow that brushed her calves as she walked through it. Butterflies and dragonflies flitted among the seed heads. What a shame to mow all these pretty wildflowers! She took pictures anyway, and of the weedy driveway, which would probably get doused with toxic chemicals, and sent them to Beatriz.

By the time she got back to the palace it was midafternoon, and she worried that Rigo would be upset that she'd neglected her duties. She headed into his office as soon as she returned. He sat behind the desk buried in a pile of papers. "Place still standing, is it?" He didn't look like he cared much one way or the other.

"It's lovely there. So peaceful. And so many wildflowers! You should see all the butterflies."

"I imagine the family will want to evict them to make way for the coroneted heads of Europe," he said drily. "And they can do whatever they like as far as I'm concerned."

"I'll let Beatriz know." She managed a brave smile. "Should I tell them I need to get back to my work?

"Absolutely, but first there's something I need to ask you."

"What?" Her pulse ratcheted up for no reason at all. His stare had a way of pinning you to the spot.

"Did your father ask you to take the job here?"

5

"Uh." Bella froze. She felt her face heat and prayed it wasn't turning bright red. "What?"

She was a terrible liar.

"He told me about the job. He didn't beg me to take it or anything." More of a strong suggestion.

"Has he shown an interest in the work you're doing?" She could swear Rigo's eyes narrowed slightly. Why did her heart feel as if it was about to burst out of her chest?

She shrugged. "Why would he? He has his own concerns."

"Concerns that we are currently investigating." Rigo leaned forward and put his elbows on the desk. "Be sure to let me know if he shows an interest."

"I will." She attempted a thin smile. As if she would put this arrogant prince's needs above those of her own father. He obviously had no conception of how loyalty worked. Her dad might not be the warmest guy in the world, but he was the only family she had left and she wasn't about to betray him.

"I need you to invite several individuals to the palace for an interview. We're looking for information that can help us solve the murders."

"Are they suspects?" She didn't much like the idea of making contact with hardened killers. What if they took a dislike to her?

"No. They're more…persons of interest. Your father is one of them." He shoved the printed list at her. "This list is confidential and does not leave this room. Please call each one, introduce yourself—as your father's daughter as well as an employee of the palace—and invite them here at the time and date printed by each name."

"No problem." She recognized every name on the list. Four of them were close friends of her father and the others were equally well-known members of the local upper crust. Not at all scary, thank goodness. "Who will they be meeting with?" She was sure at least one of them would want details.

"Me."

"I'll call them right now."

"Call your father today, then call the rest tomorrow."

She frowned slightly. Wouldn't it be more efficient to call them all at once? Still, it wasn't her job to argue. "Okay. Should I use my own phone?"

"Uh, yes. Why not?"

She pulled out her phone. Rigo sat watching her from behind the desk. Was he going to keep his grim gaze on her while she made the call? She hoped not. It was hard enough to sound natural with her dad sometimes anyway. "I'll call him right now, then, shall I?"

"Please do." He went back to his papers.

She sucked in a breath and dialed.

Uncharacteristically, her father answered right away. "What's going on?" he asked, before she could even say hello.

"I'm at the palace, standing in Prince Rigo's office, and he's asked me to invite you in for a…meeting, on Thursday at ten o'clock. Can I tell him that's okay?" She wanted to get it all out before he had a chance to ask probing questions that would be awkward to answer in front of Rigo.

She stood facing away from her boss, but she could swear she felt his dark gaze burning two holes in her back. Just being in the same room with Rigo made her jumpy and awkward.

Her dad was taking a very long time to answer. "Dad?"

"I'm checking my calendar. Thursday at ten. Can we move it to eleven?"

She didn't have to ask Rigo. "No. It has to be ten."

"I suppose I'll have to move a few things around then. I'll be there."

"Great. Thanks, Dad. I suppose I'll see you when you're here." She hadn't seen him since she moved into her own place. He'd been traveling, he said.

"I look forward to it, my dear." She wondered if he imagined someone was listening over a speakerphone. That wasn't usually how he spoke to her.

She resisted the urge to tease him. "Me too."

They said their goodbyes, and she hung up.

She turned triumphantly to Rigo. "That went well."

"Indeed." His eyes were smiling—for once—

which gave her a weird thrill of satisfaction. "I look forward to meeting him."

"It's odd that you've never met before, really."

"If I lived here I might have, but I left Altaleone for university and I've been away ever since."

"Didn't you miss it? I've lived abroad a lot too, but I miss home terribly when I'm away. It reminds me of my mom, because I lived here until she died. I still miss her every day. Then there's something about being surrounded by mountains that makes me feel like the universe is giving me a hug." As the last words came out of her mouth, she realized Rigo probably wasn't the ideal audience for them and wished she could shove them back in.

But the smile in his eyes deepened, even if there still wasn't one anywhere near his mouth. "That's an interesting way of looking at our rather forbidding landscape."

"Forbidding? The mountains are steep, but we have lush pasture, streams that flow all year round, and the prettiest villages and hamlets anywhere in Europe."

"I want to appoint you head of the tourist board." She could swear one corner of his mouth was attempting to lift slightly.

"Is there one?"

"I have no idea."

"I guess I'd better stick with being a lady-in-waiting."

A tiny crease formed in his brow. "That's such an old-fashioned title. We should choose a more appropriate one."

"Something vague and meaningless like…executive associate."

His mouth did lift, and a deep dimple appeared in one cheek. "Exactly."

"I think I prefer lady-in-waiting. It goes better with my taste in lacy dresses." She glanced down at the pretty dress she'd upcycled from an old evening dress she'd found in a Zurich thrift shop. "And Squiggles likes it better too."

He glanced dubiously at the bag hanging from her shoulder. "At least he's stopped shrieking."

"He's adapted well to palace life. I think he enjoys being in the thick of things. It is lovely here. And everyone's so nice." *Except you.* But Rigo wasn't being too beastly today. "I really appreciate your letting me bring him to work. Not everyone would be so understanding."

"I can imagine."

Bella was back at home putting out food for the dogs when her phone rang. "Hi, Dad."

"You're alone?"

"Yes. Except for the animals of course. You know I'm never really—"

"What the hell is this inquisition tomorrow about?"

"I don't really know. They have me going through old tax returns from decades ago, but I'm not sure if it's related to that at all."

"Tax returns? Personal tax returns? That's not legal."

"Not personal. Corporate returns. So far it's been the Altacord corporation."

She heard her dad flick his cigar lighter and draw in smoke. "What does that have to do with the murders?"

"I have no idea. Seriously, don't worry about it. Everyone at the palace is so nice. I'm pretty sure they just want to pick all of your brains for ideas about who could be behind the murders."

"What do you mean all?"

"There was a list of names." She rattled off the ones she could remember. She knew several were friends or associates of her father's.

"Everyone on that list was already asked to come in and be questioned, and they all said no."

"Well, tomorrow I have the unenviable task of asking them again. Why don't they want to come in? Surely it's just being a good citizen to help your country solve the murder of your queen and her son?"

Her father was silent. "Smells like a fishing expedition to me."

"I don't imagine that they think any of you are guilty. They're at a loose end and want your insight. You will come, won't you?"

"Naturally. I don't want to upset their royal majesties."

"I thought you were good friends with crown prince Emil before he was killed." Her dad's reluctance was odd, considering they were old hunting buddies.

"I was. I miss him. He'd never have had the nerve to call the entire Cross of Blood on to the carpet."

"Cross of what?"

"Nothing." She imagined him puffing on his cigar in the pause. "I'll be there. Who will I have the pleasure of talking to at the palace."

"Rigo. He's my boss. Or at least so far he is."

"The lawyer prince." She heard a sneer in her father's voice.

"Yes. He practices law in New York. He's only back here to unravel this mess."

"He probably bought his degree and maintains a firm just for something to do between sailing competitions."

She laughed. "Oh, no. You've got Rigo very wrong. In fact I'd say he's the exact opposite. He's so afraid that people will think that about him that he's possibly the most demanding, rigorous, and respected lawyer anywhere. Did you know he's never lost a case?"

"Fabulous."

The next morning she headed in bright and early, but she had barely sat down with her files when she felt Rigo's tall, shadowy form looming over her. Her whole body reacted to his presence. "Morning," she said cheerily, trying to act natural.

"Did your father call you last night?"

"He did, actually." Was there anything wrong with that?

"And you told him the names of the other people on the list?" He lifted a brow slightly.

He'd said the list wasn't to leave the room. But he hadn't forbidden her to discuss its contents. "Yes."

"Good. I think you'll find they'll be ready to talk when you call them this morning."

She frowned. "You sound like they're all talking to each other. Like there's some kind of conspiracy."

"A conspiracy. Hmm. Interesting idea." His

inscrutable expression irked her. Was he poking fun at her?

An ugly sensation clawed at her chest. "You don't think my dad had anything to do with the murders?" She knew it was impossible, but she didn't want Rigo getting any ideas.

"Do you?" Those cool dark eyes peered into her soul.

"Of course not! Why would my father want to kill his close friend?"

"Your father was close to mine?"

"Yes. They hunted every week in season. I know my father misses him."

Rigo seemed to file that information away mentally. She hoped the connection would be beneficial to her father, not the opposite.

"Have you ever heard of the Cross of Blood society?"

"Cross of…" She trailed off as she remembered her father using that phrase on the phone. "Is it related to any of this?"

Rigo stared at her. She felt her pulse quicken as he simply watched her expression, maybe hoping it would somehow betray her. Her heart beat faster, and she could feel heat rising up her neck. She was starting to feel like a defendant in the dock.

"I think it might be."

He turned and left the room before she could think of anything intelligent to say. Did this mean he thought her father was involved in a conspiracy among the elite members of Altaleone society? What would they gain from the murder of their queen and her immediate heir?

And did Rigo think she was involved?

6

Darias and Rigo drove out to the old hunting lodge on the pretext of deciding what renovations were needed, but mostly to get away from any prying eyes and ears at the palace. His neck started to ache as he drove up the driveway. "I hate this place."

"Why?" Darias looked surprised. "It's not that bad."

"It's where I caught Dad with you-know-who."

"Are you still hung up on that? It was more than a decade ago."

"He cheated on our mother. Don't you think that's despicable?"

"Yes, but he's dead and I've moved on."

They drove up the long weedy driveway. Darias could remember that day like it was yesterday. He'd wanted to walk in the hills and think over something—he had no recollection of what—and when he arrived at the house he'd seen her small sports car in the drive next to his dad's car.

And she'd done it because of him.

"So this Bella—" Darias pulled up in front of the house. "Do you trust her?"

"I don't trust anyone. You know me." Bella was

far too "sweet" to be believed. And she thought that innocent smile and guileless manner had him eating out of her hand. She couldn't be more wrong. "But she's proving useful. I had her call to invite her father in for an interview. Last time he was asked in for an interview his lawyer got him out of it. I thought I'd have to spend months finding legal grounds for a subpoena, but all I needed was Bella. Sometimes the personal touch works a lot faster than the iron fist of the law. I'm hoping word spreads through the group and they decide to play nice. That will save a lot of time and aggravation."

"That's a plus. But don't you worry that having her in the house risks leaking information that makes us vulnerable?"

"We all know better than to reveal anything critical. Which would be more of a danger if we actually had any information." Rigo shrugged. "I'm just pulling threads here and there and hoping the garment unravels." They'd climbed out of the car, and Darias started walking toward the steps. Rigo recoiled. The events he'd witnessed here had driven a wedge between him and his father that was still in place when he died. It had also permanently soured his view of the institution of marriage and the idea of romantic love in general. "Do we have to go in?"

"Come on, Rigo. It was ancient history."

"Not to me. I told Dad—later on—that she'd told me that if I wouldn't sleep with her she'd seduce my father. I thought it would make him see sense."

"He didn't believe you?"

"No." Rigo should his head. Anger pulsed through him, heating his blood. "He thought she was madly in love with him and that I was jealous. He believed...*her* over his own son."

"I can see how that could sting, but forgiveness is divine and all. Your holding a grudge doesn't help anyone."

"I'm not holding a grudge. I'm entirely rational. He betrayed our mother."

"Whatever happened to her, anyway?"

"No idea and I don't want to know." Rigo walked into the gloomy foyer, trying to banish the images of his father naked in the arms of the younger woman. Betraying his wife and the mother of his children, and unapologetically refusing to stop.

At least his mother never found out. Or any of their other siblings. He'd confided in Darias so he wouldn't explode, but otherwise he'd kept his father's sordid secret to himself.

"When did they break up, though?" Darias frowned. "I'd all but forgotten about her. What if they were still together? Could she be involved in the murders?"

An icy chill slithered down Rigo's spine. He looked at Darias. "Damn. You're right. We need to investigate her." Every cell in his body shrank away from the prospect of even uttering her name. "Gibran doesn't know about her?"

"I don't think so. No one knows about her except you and me."

"Then don't tell anyone. I'll handle it myself."

Bella was in the palace garden letting Squiggles

walk around on his harness when she noticed Rigo thundering toward her across the lawn looking harder and gloomier than ever. What was eating him anyway? He had a charmed life as a handsome prince with more money than God, and he walked around like everything wrong in the world was his problem. What a waste!

"Hi." She smiled and waved, hoping she wouldn't get in trouble being away from her work. Even ferrets needed to pee sometimes. "I'm through the first box of Altacord returns, and I've started on the second."

Rigo glanced around, possibly looking to see who could hear. Should she not have said that aloud? She didn't think anyone was within earshot.

His stony expression softened very slightly—like from granite to marble. "Did you find anything unusual?"

"Only what I told you before about the amounts being unimpressive. I suppose all these people have other businesses too, but two of the years the company actually declared a loss."

Rigo frowned. "Good work."

"What does it mean?"

"Probably nothing." He studied her for a moment, making her stomach tighten. "What do you think it could mean?"

She shrugged. "They're lucky to still be in business?" She couldn't even pretend to be interested in corporate profits from the late 1960s. "Did you see there's a golden eagle nest in this tree?" She pointed up at it—a huge nest high in the branches of a tall fir. She could barely take her eyes off it.

His eyes swiveled to the tree, and she suddenly regretted mentioning it. He'd probably want to cut it down. "Golden eagles don't nest in Altaleone."

You're not supposed to argue with your boss. She couldn't help it. "Apparently this one does."

"It must be an osprey or a buzzard." He peered at the nest.

"I've been watching it for a while. The mother is sitting on the nest. You'll see her head when the father comes back with food for the babies."

Rigo's eyes hadn't left the nest. "There are nestlings in there?" He sounded like he was cross-examining the defendant.

"Two. Maybe more."

"I need my binoculars." He dashed off across the lawn before she could say anything. She gathered Squiggles up and put him in her bag and was about to head back into the house when Rigo came sprinting back from the palace, binoculars in hand.

She fought the urge to laugh. He looked so funny in motion, with his deadly serious expression and his muscles pumping. Like a legal superhero.

Which, according to his reputation, he was.

He swept the binoculars up to his eyes—she almost had to press her hand to her mouth to keep a laugh in—and peered through them like he was checking the horizon for pirates. "Good Lord. It *is* a golden eagle."

Ha.

"One hasn't been sighted nesting in Altaleone since 1954. They were almost extinct in the whole region at the beginning of this century."

"There's an older nest in that tree over there.

Could be their nest from last year." She pointed to a ragged nest high in another majestic fir.

He swung his binoculars around and stared at it. "They could have been nesting here in the palace gardens for years, and no one cared enough to notice."

"You're the only bird-watcher in the family?"

"Yes." He pulled the binoculars down and stared at her. "And I might have flown back to New York without even seeing it if it wasn't for you."

"You're welcome." She smiled a genuine smile. He seemed so totally poleaxed and delighted by the discovery. For a half second she almost liked him. "I enjoy watching raptors, as long as I'm not letting Sapphire play on the lawn at the time."

"Who's Sapphire?"

"My rat."

"Of course." She could swear a faint ghost of a smile almost traveled across his lips. Shame he was so good-looking. Her body had an unprofessional reaction when he looked at her like that.

She probably needed to try dating again but the thought terrified her. It was much safer to stay home alone with her animals on evenings and weekends, except that sometimes her body sent up signal flares of distress—like now, when Rigo raised his hands to shade his eyes, which pulled his shirt material tight over the thick muscle of his broad back.

Why did a lawyer have a muscled back anyway?

She dragged her eyes away, determined not to notice the taper of his waist or the tight curve of his backside.

He's your boss.

I know.

"I should get back to the files." Poring over yellowed tax documents should kill this unfortunate state of arousal. "Oh, and I called the other people on the list this morning and they can all come."

He spun around so fast she almost didn't notice the way his muscles rippled under the shirt. "All of them?"

"Yup." She felt a flare of pride.

His habitually stony face had an eerie glow to it. "Bella, I think I love you."

7

"Are you busy?" Rigo's gruff voice made Bella jump. She'd been lost in a reverie that had nothing to do with Altacord's 1983 tax return and everything to do with her animal sanctuary plans.

"Yes?" She resisted the urge to add *your majesty*.

"I have a research project for you."

"Oh?" Somehow she had a feeling it would involve researching her father. Luckily, nothing at all interesting or unusual had showed up in the paperwork.

"Can you come into my office?"

She frowned, rising from the table. It must be fairly top secret if he didn't want the staff to overhear.

She followed him down the wide hallway past portraits of his distinguished ancestors. Rigo walked like a panther on the prowl. No wonder he scared the heck out of opponents in court.

He let her go in first, then closed the door behind him.

She sat down opposite his chair at the desk. "What kind of research?"

"I need to find someone. A woman. She might be living in Altaleone, or she might have moved."

A muscle twitched in his jaw. He looked even more grim than usual. "Her name is Francine Petrie." He spelled it out, and she wrote the name on the notepad in her phone. "She calls herself France for short.

She waited for him to give her more information to go on, a picture perhaps. He didn't.

"How old is she?"

He inhaled and shrugged. "About forty? I'm not sure. Woman can so easily lie about their age."

"What does she do?"

The shadow of a scowl crossed his lips. "Prey on rich men." He shone his unforgiving gaze on her.

"I can tell you don't like her."

"I could care less about her one way or the other. I simply need to know where she is and what she's doing."

"As part of the investigation? Is she a suspect?" She liked that idea. Then maybe he'd forget his dumb idea that her father or his friends were involved.

"Everyone is a suspect."

"Even me?"

"Especially you." He didn't smile, but she could swear she saw a teeny twinkle of…something in his dark eyes.

"I don't know how to prove my innocence. It's hard to prove a negative."

"Then you'll just have to find the real murderer, won't you?"

"And you think this woman could be her?"

"No, but I can't completely ignore it as a possibility."

"Who is she? How does she fit into the picture?"

"That is…none of your business." He rose to his feet. "You can go back to your files now."

Summarily—and rudely—dismissed, Bella took her time standing up. "You want an address? A phone number? Her head on a platter?"

His brow lifted slightly as she offered option number three, and she had a feeling he'd rather like that one. Which intrigued her. What had this woman done to piss Rigo off so royally?

"Her address would be adequate."

"I don't want to be adequate." He was silently ushering her out the door. She couldn't resist teasing him. "I aim to be impressive."

"Good. Then do it today."

He closed the door behind her, staying in the office. At least she'd managed to make him smile. Well, almost smile. She'd take her victories where she could get them. Her father was coming in for his interview tomorrow, and she wanted Rigo to feel favorably disposed toward her family.

She could probably Google this woman and find her address in less than a minute. Nothing was private anymore. She sat down at her table of files and opened the browser on the laptop. Squiggles had grown anxious and fussy in her absence so she fished him out and draped him over her lap.

"Francine Petrie." She murmured the name as she typed it into the search engine. Then glanced over her shoulder to see if anyone had heard her. She really should be more circumspect if she was to be an impressive lady-in-waiting.

Nothing came up.

"Nothing? How is that even possible?"

She tried France, then Ms. F. Petrie. No Facebook page, no Twitter, no Instagram. None of those services offering to show her Ms. Petrie's arrest records. No cheerful listing of her five previous addresses or her open debts or any of that other fun stuff that was readily available online.

"Now what?" She could hardly go back to Rigo and immediately admit failure. She needed this job to help get her sanctuary off the ground.

Which meant she had to locate Francine Petrie come hell or high water.

Back at Bella's rented flat the animals were delirious with joy at her return—as usual. That never happened with humans, did it? There was an envelope pushed half under her door about an elderly cat whose owner had died needing a home. Clearly word about her was getting around. And now Ari would have a feline friend.

Except that she wasn't sure what the landlord would do if he found out.

Oh, well, she'd come here to rescue animals, not make landlords happy, and she was very careful to keep the place clean and odor-free. She phoned and the person agreed to bring the cat over that night with its bowls and toys.

As she arranged their dinner she racked her brain about how to find Francine Petrie. If she weren't working for Rigo and the royal family, she'd ask around town. That was the best way to get information in Altaleone. It was a small enough country that people often knew of one another even if they'd never met.

Everything seemed so cloak-and-dagger at the palace, and she'd signed a lengthy agreement promising not to reveal palace business or the royals' private affairs to anyone. She'd probably already said too much to her dad, but they could hardly expect her to keep secrets from her own family.

Her phone rang, and an idea occurred to her. "Dad! Hi, I was just about to call you. Do you know someone called Francine Petrie?"

There was a silence. She heard the familiar snick of his lighter. "Yes," he said slowly.

An odd twinge of apprehension unfurled in her belly. Should she not have told him? He was coming to the palace tomorrow for this long-awaited "chat."

Still. This was too good an opportunity to miss. "Do you know where she lives?"

Another long pause. "No."

"Her phone number?"

"Why would I know that? I didn't call to talk about the king's sex life. Do you know what they're going to want to talk to me about tomorrow?"

"I don't really know. Rigo didn't say."

"For God's sake, Bella, you're there for a reason!"

"I know. To earn money for my animal sanctuary." Ari swirled around her ankles.

"Don't be obtuse."

"I'm not. I don't know what you're talking about." Alarm prickled through her.

"I wanted you there to keep tabs on things. To let me know what's going on. Did you see anything…interesting, in the files you've been going through?"

"No. They were deadly boring. The main thing I noticed was that the company didn't make very much money, but that's hardly a crime."

"Did you point that out to his majesty Prince Rigo?"

"About it not being a crime? Of course not. I was surprised, that's all. I thought there was a lot of money in diamonds."

"Overheads, expenses, distribution costs," he murmured. "Middlemen take it all."

"I thought we were the middlemen. I mean, the diamonds are mined in Africa and sold in Paris, London, and New York."

There was another pause, then she heard him inhale deeply. "Francine Petrie had a long-term affair with Prince Emil. He maintained her in a house in town. On Alvona Street, I think it was. A yellow house with blue shutters."

"You've been there?" She was shocked.

"Once or twice. But there's no need to tell Prince Rigo that. And keep your opinions to yourself about my businesses too. I don't want him thinking I'm a lousy businessman."

She laughed. They both knew her dad took spending money very seriously. She wasn't entirely sure how he earned it, though. "I'm sure he doesn't think that. And anyway, you'll find out what he's interested in tomorrow."

A knock on the door drew her to it, and she opened it to see a blond haired man with a cat in a carrier and a big canvas bag of stuff. She took them both, balancing her phone between her cheek and shoulder and smiled. "Dad, I've got to go, there's someone at the door."

By the time she'd put the cat, the bag, and the phone down inside the house, the man was gone. She rushed out the door and peered down the street, but there was no sign of him. "Oh, dear, I hope he left some of your food so I know what it is."

She rifled through the bag but there wasn't any. And when she let the cat out of the carrier, it was black with a white belly and paws, and quite thin. She wondered when it was last fed. "We'll give you what we have, okay?"

Ari came over to investigate, and the new cat arched its back and its claws shot out. "He's just trying to be friendly, sweetie. What shall we call you?" His name wasn't on any of the items—a few worn toys and two scarred plastic bowls. "How about Martini? You look like you're dressed up for an elegant cocktail party."

Martini looked very suspicious of her. And when Pepe started loping over she could see a situation about to develop so she swooped Pepe up on her arm and headed back to his cage. "I think we'd better put you in protective custody until we all get to know each other a little better."

Pepe squawked his disapproval, so she gave him some nuts to keep him busy.

"The king's mistress?" She chewed her lip. "I wonder if Rigo knows that."

Still, she knew where she was going tomorrow.

8

Bella left for work half an hour early, leaving Martini in her bedroom and hoping the carpet wouldn't be shredded when she got back. She walked through the town, following the map on her phone toward Alvona Street.

It was a quiet, leafy street on a steep hill. The houses were old and solid, with tall stoops. It didn't take long to find a yellow one with blue shutters. It was big enough to contain several apartments so she hoped there might be a series of names next to the doorbell, but no such luck.

Since she had time she decided to hover outside in the hope that someone would come out whom she could ask. She was just telling Squiggles that they'd have to leave in two minutes when an elderly man came out with an adorable long-haired terrier on a red leash.

After making a fuss over his cute dog she asked if he knew which apartment Francine lived in. She tried to make it sound like she was a friend of hers. The man's face instantly clouded over. "She's gone, thank the heavens."

"Oh." Rats. "Do you know where she moved to?"

"Far away, I hope," he growled. "She should be ashamed to show her face in Altaleone."

"Why?" The bold question burst out before she could think better of it.

He snorted and muttered something she couldn't quite catch about minding his own business and how she should do the same. Then he shuffled off down the steep pavement with his dog toddling along next to him.

Dammit! So near and yet so far. She could be anywhere. "How long ago did she leave?"

The old man turned and stared at her for a moment, looking her up and down. She grew suddenly self-conscious of her yellow flowered dress and the vintage lace petticoat that almost touched the ground. "When her fancy man stopped paying the bills, that's when. Good day!"

He uttered the last words with a brusque finality that made her heart sink. Her fancy man? If that was Rigo's father Emil—a married man—no wonder he didn't want to talk about it. Either way, she needed to head for the palace now or she'd risk being late.

She and Squiggles hurried through the village to the palace gates, where she greeted the guards with a smile, and up the wide drive to the palace. She was rather breathless when she arrived at her dining table/desk and found Rigo's imposing form bending over the file boxes, pulling papers out of the folders.

"Morning," she said, with some apprehension. "My father's looking forward to meeting you today." That was an utter lie, but she could hardly ignore the odd circumstance of her father being subject to Rigo's inquisition.

Rigo looked surprised by her utterance. One of his brows lifted slightly, and she regretted her phony pleasantry. Those dark piercing eyes could see right through her. "I'm looking forward to meeting him too," he said coolly. His tone implied that the pleasure would be a calculated one.

Time to change the subject. "I thought I'd found Francine Petrie on Alvona Street in Casteleone, but she's moved away."

His expression darkened. "How did you track her to Alvona Street?"

Panic flared in her chest. She didn't want him to know that she'd asked her father. "Old phone directory. Out of date." Squiggles screeched from her bag. Probably playing the role of her conscience. Why did being around Rigo make her nervous enough to tell fibs?

He looked right at her, which made her soul shrink back. "Maybe check a more recent phone book." One brow lifted slightly.

She nodded. "Sure." He knew she was lying. Did they even make phone books anymore? "Is there anything else I can do for you?"

"Aren't you the perfect lady-in-waiting?" His eyes glittered with black humor.

"And you're kind of the boss from hell, but I'm trying to roll with it." She shot him a challenging stare, also with humor. He didn't like her kowtowing to him, so how did he like her being sassy?

A smile tugged at his reluctant mouth and deepened a stray dimple on one cheek, but barely managed to pull it out of its usual dour shape. "I've never been accused of being nice. In my profession a reputation for being an ogre is an advantage. It makes opponents more likely to settle."

"I can imagine." Once again being around Rigo was getting her flustered. Her heart beat faster and she could swear her nipples were standing to attention. How could she be attracted to such a beast? If he'd kidnapped her she could at least blame it on Stockholm syndrome, but she'd come here of her own free will.

Or at least her father's. "I'd better get back to work."

"Indeed."

She could feel his eyes on her as she exited, skirt swishing around her ankles. At least he hadn't said anything about her clothes being unprofessional. At the law firm she'd worked at in Zurich they'd issued a no-ruffles edict after she'd worn one particularly festive upcycled confection. What was the point of living if you couldn't express yourself? "Right, Squiggles?"

Squiggles wasn't wild about self-expression. He was clearly happiest when curled up in a bag.

Bella came out to say hello when her father arrived for his interview, then hurried back to her work where she finally finished organizing the Altacord files up to the present day. They were every bit as boring each year, with minimal to no profits regardless of what the world economy was doing. She couldn't imagine why her dad even bothered with the company. Some years it even lost money, especially in the last decade. Maybe diamonds were going out of style?

She closed up the box, saved her database, then opened a blank version of the same file, ready for her next project. She attempted a few more searches on Francine, using local church archives, and discovered that Francine had been baptized forty-six years ago and was married and then divorced—both a long time ago—but there were no clues to her current whereabouts.

Rigo's minions had already bought in at least ten file boxes from another Altaleone company called Reisener. A quick glance suggested that it was a vineyard that bottled its own champagne. Yawn! And she wasn't surprised to see her father's name on the list of directors. Double yawn.

She was just entering the details from 1971 and counting the minutes until she could go home and see her animals when she heard her father's voice in the hallway. "You'll be hearing from my lawyer."

She heard him stride across the marble floor with even more purpose than usual. Since he made no effort to come into her room and even his footfalls sounded enraged, she decided to lie low.

Rigo swept in, and she avoided looking up for a moment, not wanting to see his face contorted with rage or indignation at her father.

But when she glanced up he was smiling.

"What?" The word burst out of her mouth before she had time to think. She wanted to know what the heck he was smiling at when her father had stormed out of here in a fury.

"Very interesting."

"My father didn't seem to think so."

"Oh, I beg to differ. He's not happy about someone peeking into his private world, with its stone walls and gates and nondisclosure contracts."

Her stomach clenched. "What did you learn?"

"Nothing conclusive." His smile belied his words. "But I'm confident we're heading in the right direction."

She wanted to protest that her father couldn't be guilty of murder, but even the idea of uttering it aloud seemed to incriminate him, so she held her tongue.

Rigo left before she came up with a way to change the subject. She was trying to forget the whole exchange and get back to her files when Beatriz wandered toward her carrying a clipboard. "I'm putting you down as Rigo's date for the wedding."

She'd never heard a worse idea in her life. "I don't think he'll like that."

"I know, but we all need to walk in pairs in the procession. He won't invite someone and he'd have a fit if I set him up with some eligible young damsel, so it looks like you're the best option."

"Because I'm not an eligible young damsel?" She wanted to be clear on that. Part of her felt a little indignant.

"You're palace staff. It would be indecent of him to…interfere with you."

"Quite." She sounded as prim as she could. "So I just have to walk in the procession with him?"

"And sit next to him during the ceremony, the dinner, etc."

"Great." Her heart plummeted into her belly. Not only would Rigo be grumpy and miserable about having his valuable time wasted—the festivities would no doubt go on all day and all night—but she'd be tormented by her strange and inappropriate attraction to him.

At least his head was so far up his own rear end he probably wouldn't notice her being weird.

"Have you been to a royal wedding before?"

"I attended Emma and Darias's wedding last year with my father. I'm sure it'll be wonderful."

"I hope so. Sandro and Serena are just too stinking adorable." Beatriz's mouth quirked into a half smile. "Though all the planning involved rather makes me want to elope. Anyway, I wanted to get you on board. No need to say anything to Rigo."

Beatriz was gone before she could protest. Great. Now she was Rigo's *surprise* wedding date. That wouldn't be at all awkward...

When five o'clock finally rolled around she picked up Squiggles and headed for Rigo's office to tell him she was leaving. As she neared his closed door Rigo's voice stopped her in her tracks.

"So I asked him about the diamond mine in Africa, and he blustered a little then admitted his ownership." Bella sucked in a breath. She knew her father owned a part share in a diamond mine in South Africa. She heard another male mumble something. "Exactly. Then when I asked him about the murder there he almost turned purple."

"Guilty?"

"Of something. The man who died was their top accountant. Maybe he was about to blow a whistle. They blamed it on a local criminal gang, but it seems too convenient to me."

Bella frowned. What did a mine in South Africa have to do with any of this? Her father rarely went there and even then she suspected it was just to enjoy a safari. He'd hardly get on a plane to go kill someone.

Still, instead of knocking on the door, she turned and fled before someone could open it. She wasn't sure who the other man was but likely Darias or Gibran. Or maybe Sandro. Perhaps they all thought her father was a vicious criminal with blood on his hands. Maybe they'd talk about him over dinner, speculating on how he'd done it.

Then they'd expect her to sit next to Rigo and smile all day at the stupid wedding.

I quit!

She wanted to yell the words at the top of her lungs.

But Squiggles snuffling in her bag reminded her of how much was at stake. She needed a job to support herself and her animals and she'd better find a new one before quitting this one.

She walked home as fast as she could, clutching Squiggles to her chest so he wouldn't bump around, wondering who in Altaleone would hire someone who'd left a job at the palace because it "wasn't working out."

Her phone rang as she unlocked the door to her house. She glanced at the number then answered with a mix of curiosity and panic. "Dad, what happened today?"

9

"A ridiculous example of royal overreach. Rigo Leone's father would be ashamed of him!" Bella's father's voice boomed with outrage.

"Rigo's trying to solve his father's murder."

"By accusing his father's closest friends?"

"Did he accuse you of the murder?" She held her breath, waiting for his response.

"Not exactly, but he brought up things he has no business prying into. That affair in Kloef had nothing to do with me and he knows it."

"What affair in Kloef?" Why did she always feel in the dark about everything? "Where is that?"

"South Africa. It was nothing, really." She heard her father light his cigar. "An accountant was murdered. It's a lawless place. Like the Wild West. People are killed every day."

Bella realized she was still holding her breath so she let it out slowly. "Do you own the company?"

"I'm one of fifteen directors. I barely remember the place exists on a day-to-day basis. You need to get your boss to back off."

"But surely he'll realize you're not guilty of anything and leave you alone?"

"Unless he decides to sink his jaws into me and

hang on like a pit bull. He's a dangerous man in the courtroom. Everyone says so. You need to get him off me."

"How am I going to do that?"

"Distract him." In the pause she could almost see him puffing on his cigar. "Kiss him. Make him fall in love with you."

"Dad! I can't do that. For one thing, he's a prince and for another, he's my boss."

"He's a man. Don't underestimate your beauty, Bella."

"You can't be serious."

"To show you how serious I am, if you kiss him I'll give you a hundred thousand euros."

"Don't be ridiculous."

"I'm not. You could use the money for your animal sanctuary. You know I'm good for it."

"I thought you didn't want to support me financially any more. Which I get, believe me. I'm mature enough to support myself."

"This isn't me just handing you money. It would be payment for...services rendered."

Her nerve endings snapped in revolt against the preposterous idea. Had she told her father that she'd kissed Rigo at the airport that time? Yes. She did mention it, when explaining that she didn't think she'd get the job he was so excited about. So now he thought she could just kiss him again...

"I really can't. I'm his official date at the wedding."

There was a pause. Then her dad laughed. "Perfect. See? He's already interested."

"He had nothing to do with it. His sister Beatriz arranged it and told me not to tell him. I could lose my job."

"With a hundred thousand euros you wouldn't need your job."

Bella bit her lip. Was she losing her mind? This idea was starting to seem less insane. She was planning to quit anyway, and with this money she could probably by a small cottage somewhere in the countryside with room for the animals...

"I still think this is a crazy idea but how would I prove to you that I kissed him? I couldn't exactly whip out my phone and take a selfie."

Her father considered this while puffing quietly. "You'd have to kiss him at the wedding, in front of witnesses."

"But why? What do you get out of it?" She squinted as she tried to figure out his line of reasoning.

"I hardly think he'd kiss my daughter then send me to prison for murder." His voice sounded confident.

"You don't know him as well as I do." She shook her head. "Even if I was crazy enough to try to seduce him, what if he rejects me, then fires me?" From where she stood, that was the most likely scenario.

"I need you to try. Do it for me. He's going through the entire financial history of my companies, and you don't seem to be able to do a damn thing to stop him."

"But why do I need to? Are you hiding something?" She grew increasingly suspicious as they talked. Her father sounded like a madman clutching at straws—a guilty man. "You didn't kill his father and grandmother, did you?"

"Of course not!" Her father's voice exploded out of her phone. "But that doesn't mean I want him digging into my business, either. Staying wealthy in this era of take-from-the-rich-and-give-to-the-poor isn't easy. You've lived a very comfortable life from the fruits of my labors in the past, and you can continue to do so if you can get him off my back. If not..."

He paused to pull on his cigar. "If not...what?" Her heart pounded.

"Don't fill your head with information that can do you no good. A public kiss wins you a hundred thousand euros to fund your zoo."

"It's not a zoo, it's a——"

"I have to go make some calls." He hung up before she could reply. She realized he was probably calling some cronies to warn them what had happened. Maybe his fellow henchmen in the mysterious Cross of Blood society. They were all perfectly ordinary Altaleone citizens from what she could tell. Fabulously wealthy, yes, but hardly involved in some kind of criminal underworld.

Right?

And the idea of kissing Rigo? Ha. That would go down as well as if she tried to kiss a Nile crocodile. It was different at the airport because they were total strangers. Now he was her boss. She'd probably get her head bitten right off.

She knelt down on the floor and let her dogs and Ari run toward her and shower her with kisses, then she went into the bedroom and picked up a rather skittish and aggravated Martini. "What am I going to do, guys?"

With the money there'd be no more breaking

the landlord's rules.

And the idea of kissing Rigo again held a strange appeal. Even though they'd only kissed that one time, her body responded to him whenever he entered a room. His mouth could be hard and judgmental but also expressive and sensual. She had an odd feeling that another kiss with him would be downright explosive.

It couldn't go anywhere, of course, but if she could pull it off she could leave the palace and get on with her life. Maybe it even would get him off her dad's back. Altaleone society was small and close knit and family honor was taken very seriously. Rigo would move on to a more likely target, find the real killer, then soon enough he'd be back in New York, and she'd be running her animal sanctuary.

Then they could all live happily ever after.

Unless she blew it all—her job, the money, her reputation as a semi-sane person—with an ill-timed pass at the least romantic man on earth.

Rigo and Darias mounted their horses in their palace stable yard. Rigo's was a big silver-gray mare, and Darias was on a solid chestnut. The groom swore they'd been in regular work, but Rigo wasn't so sure. They were his dad's favorite horses, the only two who hadn't been sold due to sentimental reasons. Beatriz was obsessed with her own horse—you'd think she was training for the Olympics—and never rode either of them.

"I can't believe you talked me into this. I haven't ridden in years." He was wearing some of his father's riding clothes, which didn't fit too well.

"I want to talk to you." Darias steered his horse toward the gate out onto the lane behind the palace that led one way down to the town and in the other direction up toward the foothills and the mountains.

"On horseback?"

"Fastest way to get away from here. Our cars could be bugged. As could the palace garden. And there are certain matters I know you want kept secret."

"Ah. Let's wait until we're further away." Rigo squeezed his horse into a trot. Funny how you didn't forget how to ride. He used to hunt with his dad when he was a kid. They trotted up the lane until the horses were warmed up, then eased into a steady canter.

Soon they were racing. "Why are you so competitive?" he yelled as Darias pushed past him.

"Why are you?" Darias yelled back as he spurred his horse into the lead.

"There's no help for us. Let's slow down and talk." They eased down to a walk and gave their horses a long rein. Rigo was surprised to find he felt exhilarated after the gallop.

"Francine changed her name," Darias said, easing alongside him. "Petrie was her married name."

"When was she married?"

"Before she made her move on you. She was divorced by then. In the last year she went back to using her maiden name, Delvalle."

"How did you find that out?"

"I went through some of dad's private effects. There were boxes of old paperwork stored up on the top floor. He'd been sending money to her for years. The money went directly into a bank account, but it wasn't a direct deposit so it stopped as soon as he died. I had Gibran's expert find out the owner of the bank account and voilà. In the last year it changed from Francine Petrie to Francine Delvalle.

"I bet she wasn't too happy to see her gravy train come to an abrupt end. Maybe that's why she had to move. Bella said she was living on Alvona Street in Casteleone until recently but is gone from there now."

"I'll bet that's why. And she never came forward to ask for money." Darias stroked his horse's neck.

"That would have taken more nerve than even she has. I can hardly believe that Dad was cheating on Mama with her the whole time. Any idea where she is now?"

"No, but she had no motive for murder. In addition to losing her royal lover she lost her primary means of support. He was sending her over ten thousand a month."

"Expensive hobby." Rigo sighed. "At least she's had the decency to stay under the radar. The affair never made the press, and I'd like to keep it that way."

"Mama might not mind so much now that she's remarried. She said she felt guilty betraying dad's memory so she tried really hard not to fall in love with Amadou."

"I'm glad she found love again. She deserves it. Let's keep this sordid affair between ourselves. I couldn't bear for her to know. When Francine told me she was going to seduce our father as revenge for my rejecting her, I don't think even she knew that her revenge sex would turn into a multiyear affair."

"Seriously. Couldn't you have slept with her to save our parents' marriage?" Darias reached out and punched him on the arm.

"In retrospect that might have been a good idea," he said grimly. "But I find romance always leads to deeper and uglier entanglements than you could ever suspect. As a lawyer I've seen too much of the dark side of passion. I prefer to avoid it altogether."

"How's that working out for you?"

"I'm too busy working to waste my time flirting."

"I don't think anyone could ever accuse you of flirting. I think everyone has given up on trying to fix you up. Did you know Beatriz asked your assistant to be your date for the wedding?"

"What?" Rigo reacted so violently that his horse startled and bolted forward a few steps. "What are you talking about?"

"We all have to be paired off for some random reason to do with seating placements or walking in the parade or something. She knew you'd never accept an actual date so you'll have a paid companion."

Bella as his *date*? His hands tightened on the reins as his blood churned. "That's utterly inappropriate."

"I suppose it would be if you intended to seduce her, but I don't imagine there's much danger of that where you're concerned."

"Too right!" His pulse pounded in his forehead.

They'd be obliged to sit next to each other at one ceremony after another—all day and well into the night.

"She's very beautiful. I wouldn't blame you if you were tempted."

"Perish the thought!" He tried to blot the vision of her laughing hazel eyes and bouncing dark ringlets from his mind. "She carries a ferret in her bag."

"She does seem to be rather a colorful eccentric, but I like that in a woman." Darias stretched. "I suppose that's because I'm an artist. You'd probably prefer someone with a bun and a navy suit."

"Indeed." Rigo was fuming. "I'll have words with Beatriz."

"I'm sure you know how well that will go over. Have you ever tried to change Beatriz's mind about anything?"

"I'll simply remind her that there must be a place setting for the ferret."

Darias let out a huge guffaw. "I'm sure she'll find that thoughtful of you. Beatriz is an animal lover, after all."

"Not like Ms. Beauvoir. She bores me with stories about cats and dogs and a macaw and God only knows what else. She's quite mad. And not the most useful assistant either. She's very slow." Everything about her rattled and infuriated him. What did he care about her new cat not getting along with her old cat?

"She's sweet. We all love her. Did you know she's planning to open an animal sanctuary? We have lunch together while you're hunched over whatever you're hunched over."

"I'm still consulting on my cases in New York as well as trying to unravel this mess here."

"Any progress on the unraveling?"

He drew in a breath. Things were coming together almost too neatly. He didn't like that. It usually meant he was missing something. "Maurice Beauvoir, Bella's father, has been hiding income for decades. His companies have been running at break even or a slight loss for decades yet he's living like a king. The money is coming from somewhere else."

"Where?"

"That's what I'm trying to figure out. And I've noticed the same pattern from the other two Cross of Blood members I've looked into."

"We know about the Swiss bank account," said Darias. Their horses strolled at a relaxed walk. "Do you think they're withdrawing money from there and not paying taxes on it?"

"It's a possibility."

"Wouldn't it have run out by now?"

"Not if it's invested well." Rigo grimaced.

"Do you think Dad knew?" Darias's brow furrowed

"I'm wondering if maybe he found out and that's why he was killed."

Darias blew out a long breath. "But if he was killed by Cross of Blood members, why would they implicate themselves with the ritual setup?"

Rigo shook his head. "If I knew that I'd have them all behind bars right now. But I did find some information on a murder—which looks like a contract killing—at one of Beauvoir's businesses in

South Africa. He was questioned quite heavily during that situation two years ago. The chief financial officer was killed shortly after he started an audit of the company's finances. Beauvoir was interviewed, along with three other directors who'd had a disagreement with the CFO, but ultimately no one could prove anything. If he was involved in that murder, maybe this time Beauvoir decided to produce a more distracting scenario so it didn't look like a simple murder for hire. And with a group of them implicated—all powerful and lawyered to the hilt—he may have suspected we'd never get enough evidence to prove anything."

"And so far, he's been right. Maybe you can squeeze Bella for information about her father."

"I've been trying. Either she's a good actress or she doesn't know anything."

"You're not doing it right. You need to seduce her." Darias shot him a grin and urged his horse into a trot.

"That would be illegal and highly inappropriate." Rigo called after him.

Darias looked back. "Haven't you ever heard of kiss and tell?"

10

On the day of the wedding, everyone at the palace rushed around in a frenzy.

Bella dressed in one of the upstairs palace bedrooms, donning a gorgeous blue patterned dress that Beatriz had told her to wear. It wasn't really her style—more crisp and sleek than her usual romantic ruffles—but she had to admit it was striking. The official wedding hair team had pinned her exuberant curls into an elegant updo and attached a small navy hat—more of a fascinator, really—to her hair with pearl-tipped pins.

Right now she looked a lot more polished and confident than she felt.

She'd wanted to impress Rigo with her amazing admin skills, but she couldn't find Francine Petrie and after toiling through the files—too slowly for Rigo's taste, she could tell, and she hadn't found anything to justify all the time involved. She kept hoping she could discover some big scoop to wow him with, but it all just looked like deadly boring financial reports to her.

She had a role in Sandro and Serena's wedding as Rigo's…companion, but after that?

In the last week Rigo had been busy and

preoccupied, barely leaving his office while she was at the palace. If she didn't know he could care less about her and her movements she'd have said he was avoiding her.

If she got fired—which seemed imminent—she'd be out of a job and out of the money to fund her sanctuary.

Desperate times called for desperate measures. At some point today—hopefully her gut would tell her when—she was going to throw caution to the wind and make her move.

A friend of Sandro's called Louis had arrived from New Orleans to command the catering, and the smell of spicy seafood already filled the gilded hallways and overwhelmed the aroma of the giant floral bouquets that had sprouted everywhere.

Serena was incredibly nervous and wouldn't let Sandro see her in her dress due to the superstition about the groom not seeing the bride before the wedding. The dress was even more special because her aunt had designed it using a vast expanse of white taffeta exploding from a gorgeously fitted bodice with a scoop neckline and cap sleeves. Her aunt was fussing over the long train while a makeup artist put the finishing touches on Serena's already gorgeous face.

"You look like a fairy-tale princess," she said to Serena. "Which is appropriate, under the circumstances."

Serena shot her a grin. "Thanks. I feel like one, though part of me can't wait until I'm just married."

Downstairs guests milled about, many of them staying at the palace and getting ready to head to the church for the wedding. Beatriz introduced Bella to her glamorous mother, Lina, and Lina's new husband, Amadou Khadem, and she gushed over how much she enjoyed his concert that she'd seen in Berlin two years earlier.

Emma looked radiant in a blue-and-white dress designed by Beatriz, and Sandro and Darias—dapper in elegant formal wear—moved about greeting guests and putting everyone at ease.

Everyone put in a big effort to make Sandro and Serena's day a huge success—except Rigo, who was nowhere to be seen.

As more and more people headed out of the palace for the short walk to the cathedral, Bella started to feel at a loose end. Should she head there without Rigo and save him a seat? They'd had literally no discussion whatsoever about today's events, so she wasn't even sure he knew she was supposed to be his plus-one.

Anxious, she hurried up to Beatriz. "Do you know where Rigo is?"

"Knowing him he's probably in his office with his head in some papers."

"I checked there already."

"Let's see…where would he hide?" Beatriz pressed a finger to her lips. "Try his bedroom. It's up the stairs and three doors down on the left."

"Okay." The idea of knocking on Rigo's bedroom door—or even of knowing where his bedroom was—made her feel awkward. What if he was in the middle of something…personal?

She climbed the stairs slowly, turning her head back to scan the crowd below in the hope that he'd miraculously appear. The hallway upstairs was empty, with everyone now either downstairs or headed for the village. Serena was riding there with her parents in a beautiful coach pulled by four white horses.

Bella approached the door with trepidation. Why did her dad have to challenge her to kiss Rigo? She felt awkward enough around him already. Besides, she'd already kissed him once for her own less-than-honorable purposes. It was a ridiculous idea, and she wasn't going to do it. She must have been out of her mind earlier to think she'd even attempt it.

She knocked gently on the door. "Rigo?"

"Who is it?"

"Uh, it's uh…" her name temporarily escaped her. Was he naked in there? Or maybe half dressed? "Everyone's heading to the church. Beatriz told me to get—"

Before she could finish her sentence, the door swung open to reveal a disturbing vision of Rigo dressed in the same elegant gray suit and cravat as his brothers—more handsome and irresistible than ever.

Maybe I should kiss him. The idea crowded her mind.

She chased it away. She had to kiss him in public or it didn't count.

I'm definitely not going to kiss him. She realized she was just standing there, blocking the doorway and staring at him. "Uh, did anyone tell you that you and I…that we're…that…"

"They did," he said grimly. "I hope you're not too offended. I had nothing to do with it."

Of course he didn't. She realized as he said it

that she'd cherished a foolish fantasy that he might have requested her at his side.

She pulled herself together. "I think it's my job to make sure you show up."

"Where's your ferret?" He looked for her bag.

"My neighbor Marie is looking after Squiggles today. Do you miss him?" She headed out into the hallway, hoping he'd follow without further coaxing.

"Unquestionably. What a shame that he'll miss the ceremony."

"I don't think he'd like all the crowds. He's a very retiring ferret."

Rigo walked a few steps behind her, and she could swear she could feel his gaze zeroed in on her backside. Which probably didn't look half bad in this very fitted dress. She made a concerted effort not to sway her hips.

Only a few stragglers now remained downstairs, possibly security personnel cunningly disguised as wedding guests. "I think we're supposed to walk," she offered, as they headed outside.

"Were you hoping for a carriage ride?"

"Who wouldn't?"

"You look very pretty in that dress."

His unexpected words hit her like a blow. "Oh. Thanks!" She scrambled to act normal, which meant at least slightly snarky. "Does that mean I usually don't?"

"You fit right in here in Altaleone with all your romantic ruffles and knee-high lace-up boots. I feel like I'm back in another century."

"You hate that, don't you?" She was genuinely curious how he felt about Altaleone.

"I don't know." He frowned, looking down the drive as they walked. "I thought I did, but there's something about the place that's so peaceful. Being here puts things in perspective. In New York every minute seems vitally important. Here, where families have lived in the same spot for hundreds of years and cows have pedigrees as long as humans, our day-to-day panics and worries don't seem as pressing.

"You sound like you're ready to move back here and become a shepherd or something."

"That would be a sad waste of my law degree."

"Why did you study the law?" Again, she was genuinely curious.

He shoved a hand through his hair as if he needed a moment to think. They were almost down the driveway, passing through the tall gates that led out toward the village. "Growing up here where everything is set in stone and things are the way they are because they've always been like that, I found myself questioning everything. Once I got out into the outside world I could see there were many injustices that needed to be addressed, and I knew the law would be the best way to do that."

"So you're kind of a superhero in a suit."

"Only when I win."

"I heard you always win."

A tiny smile tugged at his mouth. "As soon as I win one case there's another waiting. Do you know how many refugees there are in the world right now looking for a place to call home?"

"More than at any time since the end of World War II."

"Yes. And while they're still waiting, and people

abducted by human traffickers are still hidden away, and innocent people are locked up in prisons, I'm impatient to work."

"When you put it that way this enormous and carefully planned wedding must seem like a huge waste of time." They left the palace grounds and entered the village, where they could see long lines of people filing into the ancient cathedral.

"That would be my New Yorker perspective, but my Altaleone brain reminds me that it's a beautiful occasion in the lives of two special people and it makes good sense to help them celebrate it."

"So Altaleone makes you want to stop and smell the roses."

"Or the edelweiss. The ugly truth is that problems will always be piling up in my inbox, and I'm betraying my family and friends if I ignore them to focus on the needs—even the urgent needs—of strangers all the time."

"Well, I think you're a hero." His words had humbled her. "I wish I was a better assistant. I know I'm not that good."

He didn't respond immediately, which made her realize she'd been fishing for compliments. Idiot! She should have kept her incompetence to herself.

She tried to join the end of the line, but a well-dressed usher approached them and gestured for them to come past the crowd and up to the front of the church.

"It seems that animals are more your passion than filing."

"Is anyone passionate about filing?"

"Oh, yes. My admin Sonia in Manhattan lives for it. She designs the labels for the files and has them custom-made. That's dedication."

The buzz of conversation about them made it easy to talk. "I admire and envy her."

"No, you don't." The usher pointed them to two seats in the front row, next to Beatriz and her fiancé, Lorenzo. "And you shouldn't. What you're doing is every bit as important to those animals as what I'm trying to do for needy humans."

"Thanks." That was genuinely sweet of him, even if he was just saying it to be nice. She picked up the program and sat down, taking a quick—and alarming—glance back at the hundreds of people seated behind them in the long nave of the cathedral.

Now would be a good time.

She opened the program quickly, cursing her mind for even straying along such a stupid path. Imagine kissing Rigo in front of all these people sitting waiting for his sister's wedding?

What would Beatriz say? A quick glance at Beatriz caught her kissing Lorenzo softly on the lips.

Great!

They were sitting on a bench, all crammed together like sardines so her hip pressed against Rigo's on one side. Awkward!

At least her father wasn't here. He hadn't been invited to the wedding itself, only the reception, which he was probably stewing about since he took his social standing very seriously.

She glanced around, recognizing a few faces in the crowd. Most were strangers. *These people must be wondering who I am.* Maybe some thought she was Rigo's girlfriend. Maybe they even thought she was another American fresh off the plane from New York like Emma and Serena.

She rather liked the idea of being a lady of mystery, even if she was really just a lady-in-waiting of mystery.

At last everyone was seated, Sandro appeared looking very dashing and excited in his ceremonial uniform, and processional music began. Serena's proud dad led her up the aisle. Two of Serena's young cousins with floral crowns on their heads carried her train very gravely and carefully. Her little nephew carried the rings on a pillow and a tiny niece was a very adorable and smiley flower girl.

Bella felt her eyes grow moist as Serena approached her husband-to-be. She'd never experienced this kind of romance. Never even been in love. She'd had boyfriends but nothing serious. It must be wonderful—and scary—to meet someone and know that this is the person you wanted to spend the rest of your life with.

She snuck a glance at Rigo, who gazed at the whole proceedings with apparent stony disinterest. He was probably ruminating over the details of some pressing legal case in New York and barely paying attention to the romantic events unfolding right in front of them.

The service took place in the local language, which was then immediately translated into English by a perky female translator, so that the many American guests could follow along. When they said their vows—Sandro first, then Serena—there was barely a dry eye in the whole church. Their kiss was so tender it made her heart squeeze.

Beaming, Sandro and Serena made their way back up the aisle together and soon the assembled crowd rose to its feet with a rustling of programs and a muffled hum of conversation.

One down! She really had no idea how many more events today entailed because she hadn't wanted to make a nuisance of herself by asking and the printed program was vague. While most of the guests filed out of the church one row at a time, starting with the back, the royal family—including her—was whisked out the side door and toward a train of waiting horse-drawn carriages. The horses had white plumes on their heads and black-and-gold harnesses.

"Oh, my goodness," she exclaimed. A brocade-uniformed footman helped her in, and Rigo squeezed in next to her. The lovely carriage was clearly designed for the smaller people of an earlier time, and Rigo's head almost touched the satin-quilted ceiling.

"Isn't this lovely?" she exclaimed, peering out the rather small window.

"I can't wait until this part is over. I feel like a sitting target. During Darias's coronation someone lobbed a firecracker into the procession."

"True. I remember reading about that." Apprehension crept up her spine. "Do you think we're in danger?"

"Probably almost every other person along the road back to the palace is hired security staff, but even they can't always be trusted."

"Maybe it would have been safer—if more boring—to go in limos."

"The Leone family does not cower in the face of aggression." He said it simply, not even turning to look at her.

"Of course not." She straightened her shoulders. Still, she didn't want to die. Who would take care of her animals? All of Squiggles's fur would fall out again, and Pepe would go back to anxiously plucking his feathers.

Rigo turned to her. "I've made you nervous."

"I'm fine," she said, trying to sound brave.

"If anything happens to you today, I'll make sure all your animals find good homes." His eyes twinkled, like he was teasing.

She rose to the bait. "What if you're dead too?"

"Then we can both come back and haunt someone into looking after them." He said it as if he were deadly serious.

Which made her burst out laughing. She could picture the pair of them—in their ceremonial finery—wafting about Altaleone terrorizing people into buying cat food. "I think you're crazier than I am."

"I doubt it." One brow lifted very slightly. That mischievous twinkle still sparkled in his dark eyes.

I could kiss him now.

Damn it, she'd like to. His mouth was only inches from hers, and the barest hint of a smile tugged at its reluctant corners.

But if she kissed him inside the carriage no one would see it and she would shock and alarm Rigo, thus blowing any chance of kissing him in a more public setting where she'd actually be following her father's suggestion.

The carriage lurched into motion unexpectedly,

throwing her against him. He flung out his arms to steady her, and they ended up wrapped around her.

Help! The warm male scent of him embraced her like the lure of madness. Why did he have to tease her and make her laugh? Rigo was much easier to handle as a humorless legal automaton.

The carriage rumbled along the road—the horses were trotting—and the seat, which must be on springs, bounced them around as if they were on a carnival ride. Rigo held her in a firm embrace, which grew more hotly weird by the second.

Oh, dear. His muscled arms felt way too good wrapped around her. His sturdy thigh mashed against the length of hers. His strong fingers pressed into her back.

"I'm afraid to let go," he murmured. "Are you going to bounce off the seat?" The bench seat was quite narrow, and Rigo took up most of it.

"Possibly." In her high heels she couldn't use her feet to stabilize herself effectively. And she didn't want him to let go. Which made no sense. Out the tiny window she watched the palace gate flash by and they trotted up the drive to the big courtyard in front of the palace.

Don't kiss him. Her lips were only a few hot inches from his, as they sat, pinned together, side by side but with Rigo turned toward her, holding her. He looked out the window. "Almost there." Then he turned to her and she tried desperately to think of something sensible to say but since sensible wasn't her strong point instead she leaned in and kissed him.

Their lips barely brushed at first—just enough to send a cascade of sensation down to her belly—

then Rigo leaned in and planted a firm, fast kiss that sucked all the breath from her lungs. Just as she was about to explode into flames of long-ignored passion, the carriage jerked to a stop and their mouths flew apart.

Before she could say something—anything—a uniformed footman jerked the carriage door open and she climbed out into the cobbled courtyard, face flushed and heart beating like it might burst into a million pieces.

11

Bella marched for the palace doors, where Serena, Sandro, Emma, Darias, Beatriz, and Lorenzo and their other siblings were already heading inside.

What was she thinking?

That's the problem, my dear, you weren't thinking. She heard her father's voice in her head. He'd said that to her more than once. Except this time he bore some of the blame. He'd planted the idea of kissing Rigo again in her head, and it had quickly grown deep roots there.

"What a lovely wedding," she exclaimed, as she caught up with Serena. "Do you need help getting changed for the reception?" She wanted to hide away in an upstairs bedroom for at least a few minutes and gather her wits before she had to accompany Rigo in the next phase of today's events.

"Sure, that would be great. This dress has a lot of buttons down the back."

By the time they got upstairs Serena's sister was there to help anyway, but Bella tried her best to be useful. She helped Serena into the gorgeous fitted white silk dress she'd chosen for the reception and helped her change jewelry and climb into a pair of fearsome high-heeled shoes.

He kissed me back.

She couldn't get the thought out of her mind. Yes, she'd started it, but he'd responded. In fact, she could almost swear she'd felt him press himself toward her, at least for a few split seconds before the carriage stopped in front of the palace.

She managed to chatter animatedly with Serena and her sister about how beautiful the cathedral was and omigosh-you're-really-a princess-now and various other relevant topics, all while wondering how she would ever manage to look Rigo in the face again.

Let alone kiss him.

In public.

As they ventured back downstairs she scanned the hallways anxiously. Crowds of people who'd walked from the church were now arriving, ready for the reception laid out in the ballroom and an adjacent grassy courtyard. Rigo was easy to spot in a crowd because in addition to being tall there was something about him that commanded attention wherever he went.

Or maybe that was just her.

She took an offered glass of champagne and smiled and greeted a few people she knew, all while sneaking glances around so she wouldn't be surprised by Rigo and drop her champagne or pass out cold.

By the time she'd made her way to the courtyard, there was still no sign of him. Maybe he'd sloped off to escape the festivities. A party for a thousand people was hardly his idea of fun. She was beginning to relax a little, thinking that she could brazen her way through the rest of the afternoon without seeing him, when Beatriz came rushing over. "Where's Rigo? It's time for the ceremonial sword dance."

"Uh…I'm not sure. I lost him after we arrived."

Beatriz sighed. "He's so exasperating! Why does he keep disappearing like this? Can you text him and tell him to get here as fast as he can?"

"Uh, sure." She swallowed and pulled out her phone. Her finger hovered over the screen while her brain seemed to slow to a crawl. **It's time for the sword dance.**

That should cover it. Then all she had to do was act like nothing happened. Maybe he'd decide he imagined the kiss.

She didn't check for a reply because Rigo wasn't one to waste time on pointless pleasantries. She did, however, become hyperaware of her surroundings—surveying every opening for his arrival so she wouldn't be caught unawares. She glimpsed a tall presence emerging from an open set of French doors and her heart seized and she tried desperately to act casual, taking a sip of champagne.

"C'mon, Bella. It's this way." Beatriz again, hustling her out into the middle of the courtyard. Were they going to make her wield a sword?

No, it was a ceremonial courtly dance, which involved the men—including Rigo, Darias, Sandro, Lorenzo, and Amadou—standing on one side, and the women—including her, Emma, Serena, Beatriz, and their mother, Lina—standing opposite them, while going through a series of formal dance moves.

No one had bothered to show her the moves, and she could tell Lorenzo and Amadou were doing their best to keep up as well. Emma whispered that she'd had no idea what to do on her own wedding day one year earlier and to just try to follow along. At least it moved quite slowly, so she tried to look confident as they stepped back and forth and bowed or curtsied, then went to meet in the middle and take each other's hands.…

Rigo's hand felt hot and demanding. And why wouldn't it? She'd kissed him—and he'd kissed her back.

She steeled herself to meet his gaze, wondering if he'd purposefully be looking over her shoulder into the far distance.

But he stared right at her, dark eyes fierce, as they stepped closer, hesitated with just a few inches of tension-filled air between them, then backed away again.

Two soldiers in ornate uniforms suddenly raised long, flashing swords into the air and held them high, forming a V-shaped arch. Rigo grabbed Bella's hand, and they followed as each couple walked through the arched swords.

The crowd applauded, and Rigo dropped her hand as if it burned him.

I'm sorry.

She wanted to say it but how could she when they were surrounded by hundreds of people, including his entire family.

At least none of them knew what had happened.

Her phone pinged, and she hurried out of the melee to check her texts.

I'm here. Did you kiss him yet?

Her father. Of course she could text back yes in total honesty, but since no one saw it, the kiss wasn't official. She glanced back to the center of the courtyard, where Rigo stood in conversation with a white-haired old man.

Where are you? She wanted to talk to him, not stand here texting in the middle of a party where she was supposed to be working, not relaxing.

Near a statue of a naked woman fondling a harp. She chuckled. She knew the one.

On my way. Glancing around to see if anyone was watching, she hurried toward the statue, which involved walking out of the courtyard and down a short colonnade. Hopefully she wouldn't miss partnering with Rigo in some other embarrassing ceremonial escapade.

She spotted her father talking animatedly to a heavily made-up woman of a certain age who seemed to be flirting outrageously with him.

"Hi, Dad."

"Ah, Bella." He kissed her three times as if they were old friends, not father and daughter. Still, she enjoyed the closeness. It was always hard to get face time with her father since he traveled so much. He introduced her to the woman, then took her arm, excused them, and led her off to a quiet corner.

"You shouldn't have texted about the kiss," she said in a stage whisper. "What if someone had seen my phone?"

"They'd have no idea what I'm talking about." He smiled. "I saw the way he looked at you during that ridiculous performance. It should be easy."

"What? He didn't look at me at all." She leaned

in. "And I already kissed him. By accident."

Her father's silver eyebrow raised. "Did anyone see?"

"No. It happened in the carriage on the way back from the church. I was thinking about how I would kiss him later and suddenly our lips were together."

"Perfect. Now it will be totally natural when you do it again in front of everyone."

"You don't believe I kissed him." She frowned. "If you did, then why do you need me to do it again?"

"I need it to be public."

"But why?" None of this made any sense. "My kissing him might actually make him more hostile toward you. Maybe he'll think I did it to try to curry favor with him for you."

"As long as it's public, then it would be unseemly for him to attack you—or by extension me. It's simply an insurance policy. There's a murder investigation going on and it's unseemly for me to be hauled in for questioning when I'm obviously innocent. I just want to be left in peace."

Bella glanced around to see if anyone could overhear. Music from the nearby courtyard drowned out other conversations, and no one was looking at them. "Is there some reason why you need one? What's going on? Did you do something wrong?" Her chest tightened as she asked.

"Of course not." Her father tossed back a gulp of champagne. "Don't be ridiculous. I just don't want him nosing around in my affairs, which are none of his business."

"So—just to clarify—if I kiss him I can get fired

today and you'll still give me the money for my sanctuary?"

His expression faltered for a moment. Then he cleared his throat. "Yes."

She blinked. "Okay." Her heart pumped harder as adrenaline flooded her body. She could find Rigo and somehow manage to kiss him in front of everyone. It would be embarrassing, sure, but as long as he didn't shove her away—might he do that? Panic surged through her. As long as he didn't, her father would be happy and she—

Her father waved at someone behind her. Then he murmured, "I'll be watching," before he moved away with a fixed smile on his face.

Bella sucked in a breath. Rigo wouldn't respect her, but then he probably didn't anyway. Her filing and organizational skills were average at best, and he'd probably be glad not to have a ferret in the palace.

The palace now swarmed with guests who weren't invited to the more intimate church ceremony but were included in the feast and reception. A bell clanged, summoning people to take their seats at the long banqueting tables set up under the colonnades around the courtyard. There was no seating plan since it had proven too complicated with so many guests, and she was one hundred percent sure Rigo wouldn't want to sit next to her, so she decided to hide off in a quiet spot where no one would—hopefully—notice her. She slunk off down a shadowy colonnade zeroing in on a seat between two older couples.

"Bella!" She jumped at the sound of Emma's voice. "Come join us."

She smiled bravely. "Are you sure? There must be a lot of relatives to accommodate."

"Don't be silly." Emma grabbed her arm. Had someone put her up to this? "Where's Squiggles?"

"He's probably busy gnawing his leg off or something. I left him with my neighbor."

"You should have brought him."

"I'm trying not to be too high maintenance."

"Are you kidding? We love Squiggles."

It was true. Emma liked to hold him in her lap, and oddly enough, Squiggles liked it too. "You're very sweet. I'm not sure Rigo knew what he was getting into when he hired me."

"Rigo's pretty uptight. I think he needs more ferrets in his life."

Bella laughed in spite of herself. "You're probably right." They approached the main family table, already filling with relatives of Serena's from the U.S. and close friends of the family from all over the world, as well as the family members she already knew.

"Are you sure?" She didn't want to take a seat that could go to someone more important.

"Sit next to me." Emma pulled out chairs for both of them. "I'm still not good enough with the language to carry on a conversation with one of the older generation so you're doing me a favor."

Bella grinned. She'd grown up speaking four languages fluently and barely even registered which one she was speaking at any given time. "It must be hard to learn a new language as an adult."

"It is. I'm grateful that most people in Altaleone speak at least some English." Emma thanked the waiter, who poured their wine. "And I'm not up for a challenging conversation. My brother was supposed to be here for the wedding, but he didn't show up."

"Why not?"

Emma shrugged, but her eyes were sad. "Who knows? He's so unpredictable. Last time he came here he seduced one of Darias's younger sisters, so maybe it's better if he's not here. He struggles with drug addiction."

"Oh." She didn't know what to say

"Rigo gave him a job in New York—a messenger for his law firm—but he only lasted three days. He's impossible." She sipped her wine grimly.

"Don't feel too bad about it. It's not your fault."

"I know. It's just frustrating. I used to say that he's the only family I had left, but that's not true anymore. I have a big, warm, wonderful family, and I should stop stressing over him."

"Cheers to that." Bella lifted her glass. "Hopefully, he'll settle down soon, but he's an adult so you have to let him live his life."

"I just feel bad. Everyone's put so much effort into him. Darias paid a fortune for him to go to rehab, and then Rigo giving him a job.... You're surprised by that, aren't you?"

"I am. I shouldn't be, though. He seems to devote his legal career to helping those in need."

"I suspect that on the inside he's not has flinty hard as he'd have us all believe."

"Don't be so sure." Bella lifted a brow. "He's a bit of a slave driver. I wish I was faster but then I might make a mistake."

"You're being wasted shuffling papers. I hope

you get to open your animal sanctuary soon."

"Me too." Emma had no idea that if things went as planned today, she'd have the funds ready to go.

They chattered about inconsequential things for the rest of the meal. Rigo was seated about twenty people farther down, nearer to Serena and Sandro, and didn't turn to look at her once.

When the speeches started she snuck an occasional glance at him, careful to quickly avert her gaze any time he moved.

A very handsome man called Zadir Al Kilanjar had everyone laughing when he took credit for Serena and Sandro meeting because they were accidentally double booked in his beach house over Christmas. And then again when he said that everyone tended to assume that his wife and Sandro's knew each other because they were both African American, so thankfully after this visit, they would. Zadir's wife, Ronnie, was lovely, but Bella could tell she was shy and rather overwhelmed by the large Leone clan, so she made sure to smile at her warmly.

Bella rather hoped the speeches would go on forever, so she wouldn't have to face the next part of the day's events—in which she would have to somehow kiss Rigo—again.

12

The sun was setting by the time people finished their wedding cake and rose from the tables to dance. She'd have to keep an eye on Rigo and make sure he didn't slip off somewhere. She could feel her father's eyes on her, even though she deliberately avoided looking around for him. She didn't want to be any more self-conscious than she already was.

She dreaded kissing Rigo again.

Not because she didn't want to kiss him. She did want to kiss him. Her lips still hummed with the feel of his mouth on hers.

It was the part afterward she shrank from. Where he'd avoid her—like he was now—and then quietly fire her.

The part where she'd never see him again.

She hadn't realized until now how much it would hurt to lose Rigo's respect. She'd never see another of those exasperated but amused glances. She'd never get to watch his hard mouth hitch in a slight smile that she'd coaxed out of him.

"Bella." Beatriz's voice jerked her out of her reverie. "When the music starts Sandro and Serena will lead the way out onto the dance floor, and then the rest of us royal couples will join them for a dance. It's really just so the press can get some nice clean shots of us."

"Okay." Her voice quivered a little. She wasn't nervous about the dancing. She'd taken enough dance lessons to handle a waltz or a polka or even a tango. She was nervous because this was the perfect opportunity.

To kiss Rigo and screw up her life.

No! This is how you are going to start your new life! You'll be able to buy a country cottage with a big garden and plenty of room for animals. Maybe even a field so you can rescue livestock that needs saving. It's going to be great.

She tried to convince herself, but the sinking feeling in her chest persisted.

The jazz band suddenly struck up a bright dance tune. She looked up to see Sandro and Serena rising from their seats with smiles on their faces.

It's now or never.

Maybe no one would notice the kiss. They'd be busy staring at the gorgeous bride and her handsome groom, and no one would pay any attention to the far less interesting couple off in a dark corner. Her dad would see and maybe just enough people that his bizarre plan would actually work. Rigo wouldn't be able to go after her father so he'd focus his attention on finding the real killer and everything would gradually go back to normal.

In a month or two, Rigo would be back in New York and she could forget about him forever. Right?

Everyone rose from their seats, and she finally dared to cast her eyes toward Rigo. Her heart seized when his gaze met hers.

Of course he didn't want to dance with her, but he was seasoned to royal protocol and would play the role thrust upon him. His expression remained rigid as he took her hand and led her toward the center of the courtyard.

Her palm heated against his, and she reminded herself that the sudden rush of sensation was totally one-sided. She kept her expression pleasantly neutral as Serena and Sandro twirled around the dance floor. Flashing cameras made her blink and for a second she felt lightheaded, then she took a deep breath and braced herself to dance.

It was a foxtrot. Easy enough—except for the part where Rigo put his arm around her waist and rested his big hand right above her backside. Her elegant dress was so thin that she could feel the warmth of his skin right through the fabric. It sent a thrill of awareness through her, and she stiffened in response.

Act natural! She needed to stay relaxed and act like she was having fun. She pushed a smile to her lips, steering her gaze into Rigo's broad shoulder. They moved around the bride and groom, in time to the music, as the cameras flashed and the crowd stared.

She didn't know how long they would have to keep dancing, but it wouldn't be forever.

It's now or never. She screwed up her courage and drew a deep, silent breath as far down into her belly as she could. Then she tilted her chin up—with her high heels she was just tall enough to kiss him without him bending down.

Go on. Do it.

She hesitated, lips hovering six hot inches from

his. Terror swirled inside her like those six inches were a tightrope over a boiling river. What if he didn't let her kiss him? He could push her away in front of everyone or jerk his head aside. Maybe even bite her.

The music had segued into a different tune, faster, so she had to focus on her feet for a moment to keep up.

He won't bite. At least she didn't think so.

Do it!!

She jutted her chin forward, leaned in, and pressed her lips to his. To her surprise, his hand pressed harder into her back. Instead of pushing her away, he pulled her closer. His lips responded too, softening against hers and melting her from the inside out.

The music swelled around them, drowning out all other sound. Something rose inside her, shoving her fears away and tightening her arms around Rigo. The kiss deepened and she could feel his hard body through his formal attire, wrapping around her and drawing her to him.

"Rigo!" A harsh whisper made her eyes pop open. and their lips spring apart. Her gaze landed on Beatriz, dancing close to them with her partner, Lorenzo. "What are you doing? The cameras are focusing on you and not the bride and groom." Beatriz looked appropriately scandalized.

Bella glanced around the courtyard, where flashbulbs still popped against the dark night and the dim party lighting. Suddenly it seemed like every eye in the place was trained directly on her.

Her stomach descended somewhere down near her knees, and her mouth dried up.

She risked a glance at Rigo. His face was a chiseled mask—as usual—but in his eyes she could see a fierce gleam of...something. She couldn't decide whether it was desire or sheer panic.

I'm sorry. Should she say it? She'd achieved her goal and should feel a surge of triumph. Instead she felt like she'd just betrayed her country in a shameful act of treason.

She realized that she'd forgotten to force a polite smile to her lips, and she attempted one, but it ended in shaky failure. She jerked her attention, while still stumbling through a dance, to Serena and Sandro, who whirled around in the froth of her white dress, oblivious to anything happening around them.

A flash—aimed right at her—blinded her for a moment and left hot-pink dots in her vision. Adrenaline surged through her, and she felt a violent urge to flee. She steeled herself to keep going and focused her pink-spotted gaze on Rigo's right shoulder, while attempting not to trip over his feet.

After what felt like six hours, the dance finally ended and the crowd erupted into applause. She turned to the happy couple with a big forced smile on her face and attempted to look like nothing whatsoever had happened.

I hate myself.

She'd used Rigo to earn money from her own father. How twisted was that? She had an actual job like a normal person—not that most normal people worked in a palace—and that wasn't enough for her. She had to jump into an underhanded scheme to take advantage of the most principled and careful and thoughtful man she'd ever met.

She didn't dare look at him.

But the really weird part—which gnawed at her as they pulled apart—was that once again he had kissed her back. A split-second glance revealed that Rigo was looking off into the far distance, face hard as the Dolomite Mountains. As she racked her brain for something innocuous to say, he turned left and wove through the crowd without a backward glance.

She saw Beatriz looking after him—his disappearance would probably screw up another ceremonial display of couplehood—then Beatriz's gaze landed on hers. The look Beatriz gave her almost iced over her insides.

You're fired.

Bella could hear the unspoken words louder than the music, which had launched into a fast pop tune that drew other guests onto the floor.

She realized she was biting her lip—hard—and she tried to unclench her teeth and figure out where to hide.

Rigo strode out of the courtyard, heart pounding. What had come over him?

This wasn't the first time an employee had made a pass at him. Some paralegals and interns he'd encountered in New York City could make a hardened lothario blush.

But this was certainly the first time he'd responded like a besotted lover.

He headed down a dark colonnade, away from the din of the music. He'd been shocked when

Bella kissed him in the carriage. Startled by the kiss, then disturbed by how his lips had responded instinctively to hers. He'd written it off as a fit of foolish romance brought on by the wedding atmosphere.

No one had seen that kiss, and they could both dismiss it as a transient mistake and forget it.

But this last kiss—longer, deeper, and more powerful than the first—had been witnessed by hundreds. And when the pictures turned up online and in the papers the next day, it would be seen by hundreds of thousands.

No one will care. They came to see Sandro and Serena.

He tried to convince himself, but he knew it wasn't true.

Royal romance was always a subject for fevered interest and speculation. For some reason perfectly normal, sane people dreamed of joining the "family firm," where—in exchange for giving up most of your freedom and all of your privacy—you could enjoy financial security and life in a gaudy palace.

He'd been warned about such gold diggers from an early age, as had all his siblings. Bella didn't even fit the bill, though. She was from a wealthy family and clearly had at least something of a close relationship with her sleazy father, who spent the year traveling between his palatial houses, the headquarters of the various corporations he was involved with, and the ports where his yachts were docked.

Yes, Bella had a job at the palace, but lady-in-waiting wasn't a real job. There were no promotional prospects or a clear career path to follow. It was the kind of job that a pretty young woman from a good family would do for a short time while waiting for the right well-born and wealthy young man to ask her to marry him.

And from her actions today, it seemed that Bella had set her sights on him.

Rigo reached the end of the dark hallway and turned toward the stairs, ready to take the quiet back route up to the second floor and the sanctuary of his room. He stopped and drew in a deep breath.

I'm running away.

Bella had him hiding in his own family's house. He straightened his shoulders and turned around. He could hardly escape the bizarre situation she'd put him in by burying his head in the sand, or underneath his bedcovers. He needed to tell her—in no uncertain terms—that there would be no romance between them.

His feelings for her were simple brute attraction, nothing more. She was a pretty young woman with a curvy body. She knew her assets and played them to her advantage—all while having the arrogance to bring a ferret to work with her.

He marched back down the corridor toward the party. Thank heaven he was the kind of man whose head ruled his heart and not the other way around, or he might be vulnerable to her feminine wiles. He could set her straight and clear the air, then when the press stories came out the palace press office could simply dismiss them as nothing worth commenting on.

He stiffened as the music grew louder and he had to weave his way through knots of people, accepting a glass of champagne, greeting and conversing with those he knew. All the while he scanned the room for Bella. At last he spotted her, her unmistakable curls escaping from her updo and cascading down past her shoulders, standing by a wide column, talking to someone hidden from his view.

He decided to wait silently until she was done with her conversation, then quickly and quietly make his point. He refused to let himself admire the way her dress hugged the seductive shape of her body. She'd used her looks and dubious charms on him for the last time. She didn't see him approach because her back was half turned and she was engaged in animated conversation with the person behind the pillar.

As he drew close he noticed that her voice was a half whisper, which made his ears prick with suspicion. Why would you whisper a conversation during a loud and crowded party?

He loitered on the far side of the wide column, out of sight of both her and the person she spoke to, looking back at the crowd and praying no one would come talk to him.

"So you're happy? That was enough?" Her voice rose enough that he could make out the words.

He couldn't catch the mumbled reply but notice that the voice sounded like her father, Maurice Beauvoir.

"Thank goodness! Since the press took so many photos the kiss is probably at least in the back of some of them. So I get the money?"

"Yes."

Hackles stood up on the back of Rigo's neck. Her father had paid her to kiss him in public.

He cleared his throat loudly, and Bella whirled around. "Hi, Rigo." Her voice had an edge of panic. As well it might.

"Mr. Beauvoir." He nodded at her father, who looked gratifyingly alarmed. As he should after the ugly little trail of facts Rigo had presented to him during their chat at the palace.

"Prince Rigo, what a pleasure." His words warred with the fear in his eyes.

Rigo felt a dark thrill of satisfaction. They knew that he knew. He wanted to come out and ask why Maurice had offered his daughter such a large sum to kiss him, but since there was no possibility of getting the truth he decided to make them sweat instead.

"Are you enjoying the party?" Rigo spoke slowly to Maurice.

"Oh, yes. It's a wonderful gathering." Maurice had the decency to look alarmed. "Nice to see so many old friends."

"Indeed. Old friends and old enemies." He kept his expression neutral. "Sometimes it's hard to tell one from the other."

Maurice blinked. "I'm sure everyone here wishes nothing but the best for the royal family."

"Except, perhaps, the individuals involved in the murder of my father and grandmother." He sipped his champagne calmly. "Or the intrigues surrounding the funds for the Cross of Blood."

Maurice's eyes darted around, maybe to see if anyone could overhear. "Indeed. I'm sure they'll soon be brought to justice."

"I intend to make sure of it." His suspicions of Maurice had been deepening since he first arrived.

After the conversation he'd overheard he now suspected that Bella—innocent, sweet Bella—was also implicated.

"I do hope you'll allow me to steal your daughter away."

Bella's eyes widened, and he watched her swallow hard.

"To the dance floor." He said in much the same way he might have said "to a Siberian gulag." Her response was an appropriate look of fear and concern.

"Of course," she said calmly.

Rigo stared at Bella, intending to wither her to the spot with a blaze of hostility.

Instead her clear gaze made his breath hitch. Damn her. She knew the power she had over him, and she'd wielded it cleverly.

He'd have to make sure that the blow she'd struck him came back to her full force.

13

As Rigo marched Bella to the dance floor she stiffened like someone approaching a firing squad. In the midst of the throng of dancers, he pulled her roughly to face him. Her body convulsed slightly as he slid his hand to the small of her back.

He cursed the bolt of desire that stabbed him like a hot knife. How could he still feel even lust for a woman who'd kissed him with such cool calculation?

Heck, maybe he liked that part. The lawyer in him.

He looked over her head—her ebullient hair had now completely escaped its clips and pins—and fought the tide of arousal still rising inside him. They moved around the dance floor in time with the music, and he let a pleasantly awkward silence gather between them for a moment before he spoke.

"You earned the money. How much?" He said it coolly, as if he understood everything.

Her gaze flickered with distress. "A hundred thousand. For my animal sanctuary." Her gaze darted to meet his, bright and pleading. "It should allow me to buy a small cottage in the countryside."

"How generous of him," he said drily. "I wouldn't have taken him for an animal lover."

Her mobile pink mouth quivered, like she wanted to confess all and the words hovered on her lips. "I think he just wants to make me happy."

"How touching." In spite of himself Rigo felt a teeny pang of pity for Bella. It couldn't have been much fun growing up as the child of Maurice Beauvoir. There must be poisonous snakes more affectionate than him. And her mother died when she was young so he was all she had. "And what a relief that he can buy your happiness."

She flinched. "It's not like that."

He studied her face. She was trying to convince herself. From what he'd overheard it was exactly like that. And she'd sold herself to achieve her ends. Who said picturesque Altaleone was so different from the soulless canyons of Manhattan?

"It's always been my dream to help animals. It would be such a relief to have my own place and not to have to hide them from a landlord."

He raised a brow. "You freely admit to deceiving your landlord?" The song they were dancing to grew faster, and he pulled her closer as they whirled around.

She swallowed. "They won't usually allow more than one pet. And sometimes not even that."

"And you're one of the many people who feels like the rules shouldn't apply to you."

"I hate breaking rules, but I have to follow my conscience and put the animals first." Conviction burned in her gaze and almost—almost—melted the ice that had formed around his heart.

"It seems your conscience is selective." He

pressed his fingers into her back, feeling her muscles move as they danced. "As a student of the law I find that disturbing."

She tried to shrug, but her shoulders were so tense they barely moved.

"What if your principles steered you onto the wrong path?" He spoke the words low, a half growl in her ear.

"Then I'd have to live with that choice."

Her quick and quiet response surprised him. And irked him—she showed no remorse. But she would by the time he was finished with her.

He was tempted to slide his arm further around her waist and tighten the polite vice-like grip he held her in, but his arousal hadn't abated and he didn't want to bump against her. That could prove embarrassing.

The song ended, and he let her go with a mix of remorse and relief. "I'll see you in my office first thing tomorrow morning." He turned and strode away as fast as he decently could without breaking into a run.

No doubt she thought he'd fire her. She couldn't be more wrong.

Bella's nerves jangled as she strode up the drive to the palace the next morning. She'd been tempted not to show up for work today, but that would mean blowing off the royal rulers of her own country, which didn't seem like such a hot idea.

No doubt she'd be fired. Which was fine. She'd sold her own soul for a hundred thousand lousy euros and now she could build her animal shelter, which was the whole point, right?

She tried to focus on all the needy animals she would save. With a rural property with paddocks she could nurture rescued cows and pigs and horses. She'd have room for chickens and ducks and maybe even exotic circus animals that needed a home.

It would be worth it.

Wouldn't it?

She sucked in a deep breath and tried to keep her expression pleasant as she climbed the palace steps. She could quit before she was fired.

But the prospect made her heart sink. Then she'd be betraying the family who'd been so kind to her—except Rigo, of course. No one could accuse him of being kind. But the rest of them were warm and funny and had welcomed her into their midst and they didn't deserve to have her quit.

So getting fired would be just fine.

She walked along the elegant hallway to her usual spot as if it was a regular day. But it wasn't a regular day, it was the day after a royal wedding and everything was out of place. Glamorous strangers lounged on the furniture, and she could smell a large breakfast being cooked. When she arrived at her familiar work table, it was filled with breakfast dishes and laughing wedding guests.

Squiggles writhed in her bag, emblematic of her own awkwardness. Now what? She'd have to go to Rigo's office. She approached the door and knocked, noting the way her fist shook as she raised it to knock.

No answer. He'd either been sucked into the post-wedding festivities or was hiding somewhere to avoid them. And the files she needed to work on where probably in his office. She tried the handle—it was locked. Now what?

"Bella! Come sit with us." Emma hurried toward her. "I'm so glad you're here. Yesterday was so frantic that you barely had a chance to get to meet Lina. I know everyone wants you guys to get to know each other so you can go on some of her royal visits with her."

Bella didn't know what to say. Lina was Rigo's mom—everyone's mom—and she was pretty sure Rigo wouldn't want her breathing the same air as her. And they'd all seen her kiss him. She wished she could just melt into the stone floor and disappear. "Sure. That would be great."

No wonder Rigo thought she was fake.

"I haven't seen Rigo all morning. He's probably on the phone to New York or something." Bella decided not to point out that it was the middle of the night in New York. "But that's great. He can't keep you tied up with busywork so you can spend more time with us."

Bella smiled, like she was excited by the idea, when really it filled her with dread. More fakeness, more false intimacy that would only end in disappointment and betrayal when Rigo told them that her father was paying her to be here.

If only Rigo would show up and fire her!

She helped herself to some melon and brioche at the sumptuous buffet, then joined the family at the big dining table. She had no choice but to take the open spot next to Lina.

Rigo's mom was beautiful, her blonde hair pulled back into a smooth ponytail. She had an air of being calm, kind, and unflappable. Rigo would probably end up marrying someone like her.

"Did you enjoy the wedding?"

"Oh, yes." She prayed Rigo's mom hadn't noticed her kissing him. "It was lovely. I know you recently got married yourself. Congratulations." She wasn't sure if this last part was appropriate since she knew Lina had pretty much eloped, but at least it changed the subject.

She made small talk with Lina and Amadou about the ceremony and Serena's dress. Bella had almost managed to forget about Rigo when suddenly a tall form appeared in the doorway and she felt her heartbeat slow to a crawl.

Is he going to fire me right here in front of everyone? That wasn't really his style. She heard Squiggles snuffling in her bag, which was hanging on the chair, and she stuck her hand into it to reassure him. Or maybe it was she who needed reassuring.

"Good morning, Rigo," she said primly, like the ideal admin she'd never be.

"Good morning, Ms. Beauvoir." His face had an odd expression of amusement that chilled her. "I trust you slept well."

"Oh, yes. Very well." A total lie. She'd tossed and turned all night, racked with guilt. He was playing with her like a cat with a mouse. In front of all these people who'd watched them kiss last night.

"And your ferret?" He glanced at her bag.

"Squiggles is doing fine, too." Now everyone in the room was staring at her bag.

"You have a ferret with you?" asked Lina with a surprised expression. "Can I see her?"

"Sure, though Squiggles is a male." Bella

unbuckled the bag nervously. He wasn't a gregarious ferret. Squiggles blinked in the bright light of the multiwindowed dining room, his black and white fur bright against the dark polished wood of the table.

"He's beautiful. May I hold him?" Lina stretched out her manicured hands.

Bella swallowed. "Sure." She prayed Squiggles would keep his claws and teeth to himself. Lina took him confidently and held his little face up to hers. Squiggles peered at her, perhaps enjoying the expensive scent wafting around her.

"Let me hold him," said Rigo. He reached down and took Squiggles in those big, capable hands. Suddenly Bella got nervous. Would he take his anger out on Squiggles? He wouldn't hurt a defenseless animal, would he?

She stood and reached up for him, anxious to grab him back, but Squiggles instead stretched up toward Rigo, resting his paws on his shoulder and gazing adoringly up at him. "You're a handsome fellow, aren't you? Oh, how I wish he could talk." He looked pointedly at Bella for a second. Bella reached her hands out to Squiggles, who promptly turned and bit her softly on her pinky.

"Ow!" She snatched her hand back. "Squiggles! What did I do to deserve that?"

Rigo's eyes glittered with mischief. He lifted Squiggles until his tiny mouth was level with his ear. He listened carefully as if Squiggles was whispering her secrets to him. Then he lowered Squiggles to his chest, where her ferret leaned back and luxuriated against his pecs.

Traitor.

She couldn't help smiling. "He likes you."

"Why wouldn't he?" Rigo stroked her baby with a broad finger. Rigo reached for a mini-brioche from the table, and Squiggles snatched it from him with unfamiliar confidence and took a bite out of it. Grinning, Rigo reached for another and took a bite. "We'll be in my office. Bella, please join me there when you're ready."

He turned and walked away, leaving her with an empty bag and an open mouth.

"Rigo's always loved animals," said his mom with a smile.

"He has?" Bella blinked.

"Oh, yes. I lost count of how many pets he had when he was a boy. He was always finding them somewhere. He'd bring home injured birds and squirrels and what have you, and fix them up with all the concentration and care of a brain surgeon. We all thought he was going to be a doctor."

Bella stared. Rigo was such an enigma.

"Then when he was about fifteen there was a strange case involving a stateless man seeking asylum in Altaleone. There was local opposition to the idea of giving him citizenship, and Rigo became obsessed with finding a legal precedent. Since then he's been fascinated by the law and always fighting for one cause or another."

"Sounds like a man after my own heart," said Amadou.

"Absolutely. The two of you should work together." Lina turned to Bella. "Amadou does a lot of work to stop human trafficking. In fact he recently blew the lid off a big case in France that involved someone high up in the police there. He's supposed to be keeping a low profile because that ruffled some feathers."

"Marrying into a royal family probably doesn't help with keeping a low profile," said Bella. "Though you're so famous already for your music I doubt it makes much difference."

Amadou laughed. "Nothing about our relationship is sensible, but I waited more than thirty years to get Lina back so nothing could stop me now."

Lina's shy smile and the glow of love on her young-looking face made Bella feel wistful. How was it that everyone around her was awash in true love and all she could do was get tangled up with one totally wrong guy after another?

"I guess I should go do some work." She didn't want to wait around until they asked about the kiss.

"I saw you kiss Rigo last night." Lina whispered the words with a tiny smile. "He needs some romance in his life."

Bella cringed inwardly. Rigo's mom had no idea that romance had nothing to do with it—and that Rigo knew it and was probably about to fire her.

"Oh, I don't think it meant anything. I got swept away by the romance of the occasion." She hoped her nose wasn't growing.

"Rigo never does anything lightly. You should know that by now."

She swallowed. "He was probably humoring me." She rose. "I really should go get to work. It's been lovely talking to you."

She hurried away from the frying pan, heading straight for the fire of Rigo.

Be brave. You can do this. She knocked on the

door of his office.

"Come in."

She opened the door to see Squiggles perched on his lap, still gnawing on his brioche, while scattering crumbs over Rigo and his desk. The scene was so unexpected and adorable that it almost made her forget what she had to do next.

She cleared her throat and straightened her shoulders. "I'd like to offer my resignation."

14

"Your proposal is not accepted." Rigo leveled a steady gaze at her.

"But surely you want to get rid of me?" Her hands shook. It was getting increasingly hard to remain calm and cool around Rigo.

"What I want is not a matter for your concern. I represent the interests of the Royal House of Leone, and to that end, your presence at the palace is required."

"Oh." She frowned. "Why? I'm sure you can hire another admin."

"You know the old admonition keep your friends close and your enemies closer?"

"Sure."

"That."

"Ah." She was his enemy. Or at least he thought so. "Do you really think my father murdered your family?"

"You can't deny that it's a possibility."

"Then why don't you arrest him?" Her exasperation showed in her voice. She didn't imagine for one second that her father could be a murderer. The idea was preposterous—and offensive.

"Because I'm a lawyer, so I know to wait until the evidence is gathered and the time is right."

"So I'm your hostage here, while you figure out how to frame him."

"Something like that." Squiggles stared at her over his half-eaten brioche.

"And you're holding my ferret hostage."

"On the contrary. I think he's holding me hostage." He surveyed the mess of crumbs on the papers on his desk."

Bella leaned toward Squiggles, but he chirped and threw himself against Rigo's chest. She rounded the desk and reached for him, and he lunged and bit her finger.

"Ow!" She leaped back. "You've even turned Squiggles against me."

"Perhaps Squiggles is simply a keen judge of character." One arched brow lifted slightly.

"Maybe he can tell you who the murderer is."

Rigo pulled a file of papers out of a drawer in his desk. "Read this file. It's a collection of articles and police notes about the murder in South Africa. Then tell me if you think your father was involved."

Bella took the papers, holding her arm steady so it wouldn't tremble. For some reason she had a nasty feeling in her gut. "And you can have your ferret back." He held out Squiggles, and she eagerly took him back. Squiggles snuffled a bit, but went back calmly into her bag.

"And don't think about leaving." Those brown eyes bored into her like a laser. "That would be treason."

"Would I get beheaded?"

"Quite possibly." Now she did see a twinkle of amusement in his eyes. Being beheaded probably couldn't be all that much worse than being looked down on from a great height by Rigo, could it? But then she'd leave her animals alone and that couldn't happen.

So she'd have to brazen her way through this until he got tired of toying with her. Hopefully, her heart wouldn't crumble into a million pieces before then. "Is there anything else you'd like me to do?"

"Read the file, then come back and tell me what you think."

She hurried away. It wasn't easy to find a quiet corner to sit and read, with wedding stragglers still clogging the downstairs rooms, so she ended up outside on a stone bench in the garden. The first page she pulled out was a clipping from a local paper. "Stanex Exec Murdered. Body Found in Drainage Canal." It went on to say that he'd been identified as the chief financial officer and that members of a local criminal gang were being investigated.

Ha. Her father was hardly part of a local gang. He rarely went to South Africa, and even then only to go on safari or for a sailing competition or something. But the next article said that suspicion had shifted to the principals of the company because the murdered man had been doing an audit and had mentioned to his wife that he'd found irregularities on the books.

Bella bit her lip. No mention of her father. It could be anyone.

Next she pulled out a stapled sheaf of typed pages that turned out to be a confession. Someone named John Langa confessed to hitting the dead man over the head with a tire iron and dumping him in the canal. It was grim reading, but once again, pretty much let her father off the hook...until she got to the last page, where John Langa named Maurice Beauvoir as the man who had hired him to do the job.

The words blurred before Bella's eyes. Impossible! She couldn't imagine her father on the phone with a hired killer, giving him the macabre directions about whom to kill. Still, her knees shook and she felt lightheaded. She had to put the papers down and steady her breathing.

And Rigo had read this. No wonder he thought her father was guilty of something.

The whole situation was impossible. Her father was being framed. John Langa—whoever he was— had decided to try to shift the blame from himself and her father was his convenient target.

She rifled through the rest of the papers, including internal memos from Stanex about the audit, a police letter to a local lawyer stating that excessive force might have been used in questioning Langa, and more articles about how the company was going to declare bankruptcy. The local police had interviewed and investigated her father but due to the lack of evidence they hadn't been able to build a case against him. She closed the file with trembling fingers and more questions than answers running through her head. John Langa must be lying to protect someone else who hired him, but who?

She ran into Lina and Amadou on her way back into the palace and tried to chatter politely with them about the roses in the garden—apparently they were Lina's pride and joy—without bursting into tears. She managed, then headed back inside, still attempting a smile at all the guests and staff milling about the place.

She knocked on Rigo's door with a grim sense of foreboding.

"Come in."

She entered and shut the door behind her. "John Langa lied."

Rigo leaned forward in his chair. "Possible, but how did he have your father's name?"

"The real culprit fed it to him so my dad would get framed?" Even she could hear the question quivering in her voice.

"Possible. My hypothesis is that one or more of the principals of the company were embezzling. The CFO was new and had arrived from London with a mandate to turn the company's financials around. Someone knew the scheme was about to be exposed so he decided to hire a local to kill him, maybe just to buy himself enough time for a cover-up."

"But my dad is rich. Why would he go to the trouble of embezzling, let alone murder?"

"Going to this kind of trouble might be the reason why your father is rich. You've seen the financials on the companies he's involved in. They rarely make any substantial money, and perhaps embezzling is the reason why."

"So, by a leap of imagination, you think he may have murdered your family or hired someone to do so?" Bella stood still, her back to the door, chest tight, tears creeping up on her. "I don't believe it. I don't." A hot tear burned down her cheek. "It has to be someone else."

"Then who?"

"I'm not a detective." Another tear rolled down her cheek. "I couldn't even find this Francine person in a country as small as Altaleone. I think you're wasting your time with me. You should let me go."

"I'll let you go when I'm done with you." His tone was cool, even. He talked as if he were an ogre keeping her prisoner in his remote castle.

"What do you want me to do?" She tried to sound professional when all she really wanted to do was yell at him.

"Keep going through the files just as you have been. You're more useful than you know."

He kept his stern brown gaze on her long enough to crumple her insides. Why did their last kiss keep sneaking back into her consciousness? He knew she'd done it simply to serve some selfish purpose of her own. Just like that first time in the airport...

No wonder he hated her. She didn't deserve the admiration or friendship, let alone the love, of a man like Rigo. He'd probably never used anyone in his life. He was honest to the point of blunt rudeness and clung fiercely to his principles. With his background he could be sailing through life on a yacht, but instead he was hunched over his desk defending the rights of disenfranchised strangers on this lovely sunny day in Altaleone.

She realized that she probably should have responded by now, but Rigo was already head down over a thick sheaf of papers, so she simply turned and left.

Rigo's family was so friendly and warm that it would have been a pleasure to spend time with them if she wasn't tortured by the knowledge that she'd been sent here as a paid mole—and Rigo knew it.

She'd escaped out to the garden with Squiggles for a breath of air when Serena walked by with her little dog, Lucky. "We should see if Lucky gets along with Squiggles," said Serena. "He's very friendly."

"Squiggles isn't," she said apologetically. "I don't want Lucky to get bitten."

"Rigo told me you have an animal rescue. I think that's awesome. Did he tell you that Sandro and I found Lucky tied up outside during a freak storm, about to drown in flood water?"

"I didn't know that. His owner had left him there?"

"Yup. Luckily, when we located the owner he agreed to let us keep Lucky. Which is only fair since he'd have drowned if we'd left him there."

"Thank goodness! It drives me crazy that someone would leave a dog to fend for itself in a disaster."

Bella's phone rang. "Excuse me." Her landlord. Hopefully he hadn't found out about the new cat. "Hello." She could hear barking in the background.

"Ms. Beauvoir, I am standing in the apartment that I rented you, and I am surrounded by animals that you never mentioned to me at the time of the rental. I agreed to let you keep one dog and one cat."

Her stomach clenched. That was Suki's shrill bark. "I, uh…I could pay extra."

"I'm afraid that won't be possible." He was shouting over the barking. Now she could hear Pepe's loud squawk adding to the cacophony. "I need you and these animals gone by the end of the week, or I'm taking you to court for breach of promise."

"But that's three days!" How could she find somewhere else in that short time?

"Move or get sued." The line went dead.

"Oh, crap." She felt herself sag. Then she remembered she was with a royal. "I'm sorry, I didn't mean to curse."

"Oh, please. I curse all the time. Though I suppose I should stop now that I'm a princess." Serena shrugged. "What happened?"

Bella sucked in a breath. "My landlord has discovered that I have more animals than my lease allows. He says I have to be gone in three days."

"Is that even legal?"

"Altaleone isn't the most progressive country. A lot of our laws date back to the middle ages."

"Can you stay with your dad? He lives locally, doesn't he?"

"He's not a huge fan of animals."

"The royal family has houses all over Altaleone. Maybe you could borrow one."

"I doubt they'd want all my animals in one of their properties any more than my landlord does."

"Can't hurt to ask." She pulled out her phone, and before Bella could stop her, she was explaining the situation to Sandro. In less than a minute, Sandro, Lina, and Emma were striding across the lawn toward them. She could sense Squiggles curling into a tighter ball inside her bag, as if bracing for the onslaught of humans.

"Oh, Bella, I'm so sorry," exclaimed Lina. "I know you loved the short commute from your house. But in two days all the wedding guests will be gone and we can help you move into one of our properties, at least until you can find somewhere more permanent."

Serena smiled at her triumphantly.

"You could stay in the orangerie, which is in town and walking distance, but that has no garden. There's an old lodge that's a short drive, but it has far more room for your animals to roam and there's a lovely walled garden."

Bella blinked. Lina must be talking about the place she checked out when they were planning where to billet the guests. Would they really let her stay there? "Uh, that belongs to Rigo, doesn't it?" The last thing she wanted was to further irritate or take advantage of him, and this was bound to do both.

"Oh, Rigo could care less about it. It's a bit desolate and spooky, but there are guests staying there right now so it's probably been spruced up. You could take a look and see what you think."

"I've seen it and I think it's wonderful, but I really don't want to impose."

Lina shook her head. "On the contrary, you'd be doing us a favor by breathing some life back into the place. All these old houses we own rather lose their spirit when there's no one living in them for decades."

This was all far too good to be true. "You do

realize that I have six animals. Actually seven including Martini, my new cat that just arrived. I have a rat named Sapphire." Nobody ever seemed to want a rat in their house.

"Don't worry. The place is far too big for them to destroy it easily. You can move in as soon as the guests are gone, which won't be more than a day or two."

Bella drew in a breath. It was an amazingly practical solution—except that now she'd be utterly dependent on Rigo's goodwill. Still, she only needed a place until she could buy one, which wouldn't take that long, would it?

Her phone pinged, making her jump. A text from Rigo. **Please come into my office.**

15

Bella walked along the hallway as slowly as she could without drawing attention to herself. She was trying to compose a good way of letting Rigo know that his family had offered to let her and her entire menagerie stay in his house—without even asking him.

She knocked softly on the door.

"Come in." He didn't look up. "The palace has a large hay truck that can help you move."

"You know?"

"Yes." Now he glanced up, pinning her with his dark gaze. "Fine with me. Ask your father about Africa. Watch his body language when he tells you what happened."

She frowned. "I already told you my loyalty to my father trumps my loyalty to you."

"I have faith in you." He didn't blink.

"That makes one of us," she quipped. Who was he to think she'd tell him the truth? Not that there was any kind of unpleasant truth to tell. Her father wasn't a murderer. "Besides, my father's so busy it would be a miracle if he even has time to meet with me in person."

"Don't you have a large check to pick up?" One

eyebrow lifted slightly.

"I expect he'll do a wire transfer." Did he really think people wrote checks for that kind of money? Maybe royals did. "Still, it's very kind of you to let me and my animals stay in your house."

"Kindness has nothing to do with it."

He probably wanted to keep her in his vice-like grip until he figured out a way to pin the murders on her father. She shivered. She really should hate him, shouldn't she?

"Is it okay if I go home? I'd like to start packing."

"Sure." He didn't check the time. She knew it was still early. Maybe she was testing him. "And call your father."

Bella left a message for her father explaining her proposed upcoming move and asking if they could meet. She wanted to make sure he didn't forget to transfer the money. She needed to start shopping for her permanent home as soon as possible—before the current situation blew up in her face, which it was bound to do sooner or later.

To her surprise her dad called back as she was feeding pistachios to Pepe. "Can I come over for dinner?" she asked. She didn't want to put him on the spot in the hushed atmosphere of an expensive restaurant, and he didn't enjoy tangling with her animals.

"I was going to suggest that." His voice sounded uncharacteristically warm. "Eight o'clock, if that's convenient for you."

His easy agreement shocked her—and made her a little nervous. Maybe he was impressed that she was moving into a royal palace and wondered if she might be about to become the next royal bride.

No need to let him know that couldn't be further from the truth.

"Eight is perfect. I'll see you then."

Bella drove up to her dad's house half an hour early, wanting to arrive before dark. The warm stone of the facade glittered like gold in the fading sunlight. The lovely estate—a mix of woods and open pasture dotted with picturesque stone buildings—had been in the family for hundreds of years. She'd never questioned where the money came from, assuming that—like the impressive family titles—it had been inherited and simply continued to prosper under her father's care.

Avoiding the grand front entrance and her dad's intimidating butler, she parked on the stable side of the house and entered the house through the side door. Almost immediately she heard her dad's voice and was about to call out when she realized he was speaking on the phone.

"I warned you not to trust a local. We should have sent someone from home to finish the job. Someone who knows we mean business. Now there's a loose end to flap around and make trouble. Get rid of it."

Bella froze. If Rigo overheard this he'd assume her dad was talking about the hired hit man in Africa. But most likely he was talking about—

She racked her mind...and her imagination failed her. Bella felt herself shrinking against the wood paneling.

The heavy door to her father's office swung open, sending a sharp triangle of light slicing into the hallway. She jumped half out of her skin, then steadied herself and kept walking slowly toward his door. "Dad?"

"Bella, darling." His languid greeting sounded phony. The old hurt ached in her chest. "I was finishing up some business."

"What kind of business?" She couldn't stop herself. "Some nonsense. It's so hard to find reliable subcontractors."

"For what?"

"Oh, nothing."

"Please tell me. I've spent the last few weeks going through all your business files, remember? I'm kind of curious." She steeled herself. "Is it the champagne? Or the diamond mine in Africa?"

Her dad's sudden stillness chilled her. For the first time ever she felt a distinct hint of actual danger in the air.

"Oh, never mind." She forced a smile to her lips. "What do I care anyway? I'm so excited to have the money to build my sanctuary." She inhaled slowly. "When will it arrive in my account?"

Her father closed the office door behind him and headed down the hall toward the rest of the house. "I'm moving some things around. I'll let you know when it's ready."

"I need it soon. I'm not sure how much longer they'll keep me on at the palace."

"What do you mean?" He wheeled around. "I thought you were about to move into one of their unused homes."

"Yes, but...you know how it is. They're royal and fickle, and they'll get sick of me."

"Make sure they don't."

"For how long?" Did he expect her to work there for the rest of her life—or only until the "loose end" in Africa was cleaned up?

"Until this nonsensical investigation dies down."

"You mean until they find the murderers?" It was hardly nonsensical.

"Exactly." He shone a chilly smile at her. "I asked Raina to prepare your favorite."

"Cassoulet?" A ray of warmth spread through her that he'd remembered.

"Roast pork, with the crackling skin and roast potatoes."

"Oh." She didn't even like pork. Must be one of his ex-girlfriends' favorites. That familiar sinking feeling returned. "Great."

At the dining table, under the stern gaze of her forbidding ancestors, she played at sipping her wine but didn't want to risk getting tipsy so she didn't swallow any. She talked about her plans for the sanctuary and how she would have a quarantine area for integrating new animals and a play area for prospective adopters to meet pets ready to find a new home.

Her father looked bored and distracted as he sawed away at his pork. At last he looked up. "Does Rigo have any new suspects in the murders?"

"Not that I know of. They don't really discuss that sort of thing with me." She could tell her father about Francine. Bella wasn't sure if Francine was an actual suspect or not but she was certainly a person of interest. Unexpected loyalty to Rigo made her hold her tongue

"You should ask."

"It's not really my place."

141

Her father laughed. "You're not a scullery maid, my dear. Our line is older than the Leone's."

"It's not so much that I'm intimidated, more that they're such lovely people I don't want to annoy them." *And I'm starting to feel like a traitor in their midst.* "I think I've pushed my luck far enough by kissing Rigo. Right now they probably think I'm a bit ditsy, but if I start asking probing questions they'll wonder what I'm up to."

"Good point. But do keep your ears open. What have you learned about the investigation?"

She shrugged, wishing there was actual news to share. "Nothing, really. I do know Rigo is growing suspicious of the Cross of Blood. He thinks it has a financial motive."

"Ridiculous."

"What is the point of it? There are all sorts of rumors, even that it's to provide for the royal family's kinky sexual proclivities, but no one seems to know what it's really about." Curiosity emboldened her. "You're in it, aren't you? What is its true purpose?"

His face darkened. "To protect the monarchy."

"Then it's failed, so why not disband it?" She could hardly believe her boldness. She glanced at her wine to make sure she hadn't accidentally drunk it.

Her father's bushy brows lowered further. "One failure does not invalidate a thousand-year-old institution."

"But there are hardly any members left. Most of their lines have gradually died off over the centuries."

"That makes the work of our remaining members all the more important."

"But what is that work?" She could almost feel Rigo egging her on. He'd be so proud if she could get a real answer. She realized with horror that she desperately wanted to make him proud. "Rigo thinks the Cross of Blood is behind the murders." She leaned forward, heart pounding. She could see her father's face growing redder with every word she spoke. "Is he right?"

16

"You've lived a very privileged lifestyle, young lady. You've never had to wonder where the fees for your expensive schools came from and now you're about to enjoy a large infusion of cash for very little work. If I were you I'd remember the old proverb about looking a gift horse in the mouth."

In other words...yes, the Cross of Blood was guilty. And her dad was in it. Her thoughts ran in a million different directions. "Did you know what they mean, about looking the gift horse in the mouth?" She didn't pause for him to interject, she needed to give herself time to think. "It's because you can tell a horse's age by looking at its teeth. If you were buying it, of course you'd want to know if it's five years old or twenty-five, but if it's a gift—"

"Then it would be rude to inquire about its age." Her father lit a fresh cigar and blew a puff of smoke over the ruins of his pork loin. "Exactly my point. When you have everything you need handed to you on a silver platter, you don't demand to know the provenance of the platter."

Her father was guilty. He'd as much as admitted it. Was he guilty of murder or just an accessory? And he expected her to keep his secrets from the royal family.

Her pulse hammered, and she felt her breathing grow quicker. *I've got to get out of here.*

And she had to get out of the palace—fast. And she definitely couldn't move into a royal residence when she was deliberately deceiving them.

She also couldn't take money from her father. *Ill-gotten gains. Blood money, even.* "I really should get back home. Ari needs her injection."

Her father startled her by laughing out a puff of smoke. "You go give your kitten a shot and don't worry yourself about things that don't concern you and aren't good for your health. The less you know, the better. Who knows? Maybe there's a royal wedding in your future."

"Hardly." She spat the words. "But that's not your concern either, is it?" She wanted to regret her petulant words, but she was so angry right now she could hardly see straight. She'd been defending her own father for weeks, and all along he'd been guilty.

She could never tell Rigo the truth. Blood was supposed to be thicker than water, and betraying her father would be an act worse than treason.

She just wasn't sure she'd ever be able to look him in the eye again. She rose to her feet. "Thanks for dinner."

"The money will be in your account by next month."

She wanted to throw the money back in his face, but something told her that could be dangerous right now. She could do that later once she'd figured out her exit strategy from this big royal mess. "Good night, Dad." She hissed the words through closed lips.

"Give my love to Prince Rigo."

"It's not a joking matter. I can't believe you paid me to kiss a prince."

"I can't believe you actually did it." Her father huffed out a laugh. "You have more moxie than I gave you credit for. Or more greed." His guffaw made her stomach churn.

A mistake. She was thinking about the animals, but they didn't deserve to be supported by funds from a criminal enterprise, no matter how ancient or "noble." She turned and fled down the hallway toward the side door.

No sign of his staff tonight. The dinner had been left in covered dishes on the dining room table. No doubt to ensure privacy.

She slammed out of the house and into her car, then peeled out of there—scattering gravel—as fast as she could.

The next morning Bella paced back and forth in her apartment—the apartment she was about to be kicked out of—trying to figure out a course of action.

She had to leave her job at the palace because she couldn't continue to work for Rigo while knowing her father was guilty of fraud or worse. For the same reason she couldn't move into Rigo's house. And she couldn't accept any offers of help or money from her father...

So she needed a new job, and a new place to live, preferably today.

A hysterical laugh peeled out of her. The ideal situation would be a live-in position, maybe as a housekeeper in one of the grand old houses around Altaleone—except that those didn't usually allow you to bring even one pet, let alone an entire animal rescue.

She was supposed to be at work half an hour ago, but she couldn't figure out how to face Rigo.

A knock on the door made her jump. Probably the landlord coming to remind her to get lost. "Who is it?"

"Rigo."

Her blood chilled. She hadn't even plucked up the courage to call in sick, and she was still in her PJ's. Still, she could hardly pretend not to be here now that she'd called out. She faked a cough. "Coming."

She probably looked like death anyway, so her fake illness would be convincing. She pulled open the door. "Sorry I didn't call, I—"

"What did your father say?"

"About what?" Rigo didn't even give you a moment to catch your breath. Why couldn't her father have lied? He could have protested that the Cross of Blood was entirely honorable and that he'd never done a wrong thing in his life. She'd have believed him.

But he wanted her to know he was guilty. Probably so he could count on her not to encourage Rigo's investigation. His faith in her was impressive…and depressing.

"About Africa."

"He said it was none of my business." She wasn't going to lie. "Which I suppose is true. He's very sexist. He believes women, especially his daughter, should be seen and not heard."

She hoped Rigo would take that as a reason and not press further.

Something glittered in Rigo's eyes. Something like triumph. She wanted to hate him for trying to destroy her father, but he was in the right.

I hate them both. She tried to convince herself. "I'm not well."

"Don't worry about making excuses. I know you need to pack."

She hadn't even started packing. What was the point when she had no idea where to go? Maybe she'd wait until the bailiffs put all her stuff and her animals out on the streets of Casteleone.

"I came to help you."

"What?" Shock almost made her fall off her feet. "Why?"

"Why not?"

"Uh, because you're busy?"

"I'm also aware that you are far too proud and stubborn to ask anyone to help you." He crossed his arms over his chest.

Indignation shot through her. "Me? You're proud and stubborn."

"True."

She noticed for the first time that he wore dark jeans and a casual long-sleeved gray T-shirt, looking for once less like a lawyer or a prince and more like an ordinary mortal.

Not very much like one, though. With his daunting height, flashing dark eyes, and supercilious air, Rigo generally looked more like an archangel stalking the planet than a regular guy. "Where are your boxes?"

"I'm more of a stuff-things-into-bags girl."

A half smile creased his face. "You would be."

Ugh. Why was he being adorable? Her cats—who were getting along today—wound themselves around his legs, and he bent down to pet them. She preferred him when he was giving her orders or growling about something. And she needed to get rid of him so she could make plans.

"I really don't feel good. I might get sick at any minute." With everything going on right now she might be quite capable of barfing out of sheer nerves. "I really should lie down."

"At least I don't have to worry about you trying to kiss me."

She felt her face heat. "Ha ha."

"Because we're not in public right now."

"I swear I won't kiss you if you just leave right now."

"But what if I want you to kiss me?"

Bella blinked. Rigo eased closer, sparking an uncomfortable reaction inside her. He couldn't be serious, could he?

Of course not, dummy!

He was playing with her. Getting revenge for her using him at the wedding. And she deserved it. "I don't blame you for being mad. I'm not sure I ever actually said it to you, but I am sorry." She hated the way her skin pricked with sensation whenever he came near.

"Sorry?" Amusement sparkled in his dark eyes. "I do hope not." He drifted closer. "Not when you achieved your goal so successfully."

"About that...I already decided that I'm not going to take the—" His mouth cut off her words, closing hotly over her mouth in one swift movement.

A shudder roamed through her as her mouth met his and her hands flew to his arms. Her body seemed to melt into his as rational thought drifted away. She couldn't blame him. Every time she kissed him she had an ulterior motive: escaping a crazy ex…placating her father…. Except the time in the carriage—and now.

He held her closer, her breasts crushing against his chest, and kissed her until she could barely breathe. At last he lifted his head—he was taller than her—and left her open mouthed and gasping.

He leveled a cool gaze at her. "I believe that's the first time I kissed you instead of the other way around."

She blinked. Her whole body pulsed with awareness. Everything about Rigo aroused, intrigued, and excited her. Even though she knew he must hate her she couldn't help the powerful attraction she felt in his presence. "I like kissing you," she confessed. "And being kissed by you."

She could admit it. She was planning to leave her job anyway.

"I suppose that should be a relief." He looked down on her from a great height. "That you take pleasure from kissing me instead of just taking advantage of me."

His hand still rested at her waist, and she could feel the heat of it searing her skin through her thin T-shirt. She wanted to kiss him back. To hold him tighter.

"I didn't mean to use you."

"I was in the right place at the right time." One dark brow lifted.

"Something like that." His dark gaze pinned her. Could he see right through her? Did he know she was keeping secrets from him, protecting her dad?

Maybe he felt he could kiss them out of her.

Maybe he could. "You really should go."

"Leave?" His chiseled features revealed no expression. "Because there's no one here to watch us?"

"Because…this isn't a good idea." Her skin sizzled under his touch.

"I beg to differ." He lifted a hand and pushed it gently into her hair. Which she hadn't brushed yet today. She hadn't even looked in the mirror. It was probably an unruly tangle. "I think it's time we got to know each other more intimately. We have kissed four times now, after all."

The airport. The carriage. The wedding…and now. The sensations and feelings inside her grew more intense each time. Her initial superficial attraction to Rigo had deepened as she'd learned more about him. Now admiration mingled with arousal in a dangerous cocktail that threatened to unhinge her.

She was catching feelings for him.

And that definitely wasn't a good idea. "Four times too many. It's all my fault. I'm sorry."

"Stop saying you're sorry!" His voice boomed. Tintin started to bark. "For God's sake shut up and kiss me."

He didn't lean forward and kiss her again. Instead, he leveled his steady gaze right at her and waited for the inevitable…. She angled her chin up, drew in a deep, bracing breath, and leaned up to press her lips to his.

She couldn't help it. Even if it didn't make any sense, the urge was irresistible. Maybe she was just responding to his royal command. Perhaps it was impossible to say no to Rigo, even if she knew the emotional fallout might leave her crying and shaking after he left.

Initiated by her, the kiss felt even more powerful. She did want to kiss Rigo...and she wanted more. Already her hands tugged at his shirt, her fingers clawing at the fabric and testing the hard muscle beneath.

His hands started to roam, stirring swirls of sensation. She pressed her body against his, wanting to eliminate the distance separating them, to move past the misunderstandings and confusion and the half-truths that kept them apart.

She'd been sent to him to find information. He'd employed her to squeeze information out of her. But right now there was nothing between them but hot skin, fevered breath, and unspent desire.

Her hands slid under his shirt and roamed over the warm bare skin of his chest. He caressed her breasts and backside, eventually reaching under her pajama T-shirt and touching her nipples. She gasped at the sensation.

It was all too much. Too much anxiety, too much fear, too much attraction. The emotions and sensations crashing inside her threatened to erupt into a grand explosion if they didn't...if she didn't...

Before she could stop herself she'd unbuttoned his jeans and reached inside them for the hard evidence of his desire. Rigo emitted a tight groan as she touched him. His arousal was every bit as intense as hers. Her frantic pulse, her fast breaths, the light sheen of sweat breaking out on her skin, echoed his.

He pulled off her top first. No bra. He didn't hesitate to bend his head to suck her nipples gently but firmly, making her cry out at the intense sensation. Then he knelt to lower her pajama pants—no underwear—and pressed his face into her crotch.

The shock of his cool tongue on her clitoris made her shiver. She bucked against him and had to grab him to steady herself. Just when she thought her knees couldn't hold her up a moment longer, Rigo rose up and swept kisses over her belly, her breasts, her neck, and finally her face.

So aroused she could barely function, Bella managed to pull his top up over his head and push his jeans down past his powerful thighs and strong calves. His shoes proved a sudden impediment that neither of them quite knew how to handle so he kicked them off impatiently and stepped out of his pants.

Now, completely naked in broad daylight in her apartment, Bella felt a sudden moment of panic. What was she doing? This was Rigo—her boss. *Prince* Rigo. This could not possibly end well.

But her thoughts dissolved as Rigo's hot tongue plunged into her mouth and his fierce erection pressed into her belly. Through desire fogging her brain she barely heard his gruff question: "Where's your bedroom?"

17

Bella gestured with her chin. Her bedroom wasn't ideal. Pepe's cage was in there—with Pepe in it ready to watch them with his beady eyes.

Rigo slid his arms around her and moved her bodily into the bedroom, closing the door behind them. He didn't seem to notice Pepe. Before she knew what was happening she lay on her back on her still-unmade bed, as Rigo climbed over her.

Then he stopped. "A condom. Dammit!"

She gulped. "I uh...I have some in the bathroom." A souvenir from the ill-starred romance she was escaping when she accosted him at the airport. She hadn't even been on a date since. "Let me get them."

"Don't move." His commanding tone almost made her laugh. "I'll find them."

She wasn't sure she wanted Rigo rifling through her bathroom cabinets, but you couldn't really argue with someone who was royal, a prince, your boss, and totally naked—could you? He returned in what seemed like seconds, eagerly tearing into the wrapper.

His expression was intense, focused, as if he were chasing details of the most complex legal case, except that instead he was easing himself onto the bed and down over her waiting body.

She was so aroused that he slid inside her with ease. She shivered again, a tiny moan sliding out of her open mouth as their bellies pressed together. He kissed her neck and face softly, caressing her hair, moving inside her with exquisite tenderness.

It was hard to believe this was the same Rigo who struck terror into the hearts of rivals and…well, just about everyone. Under the forbidding chiseled exterior was a man of passion and tenderness. He moved inside her with assurance and power, stirring excitement in places where she didn't know she had nerve endings, but also with sensitivity and gentleness.

As the rhythm between them quickened, she felt emotions welling inside her. Maybe it was the stress of the past few weeks, her uncertainty about the future or her surprise at the unexpected passion between them, but she found herself on the brink of losing control. She wasn't sure whether she was going to laugh or cry or scream when she found herself swept away by the crashing wave of the biggest orgasm she'd ever experienced.

She felt the force of Rigo's climax as he shuddered violently and emitted a rough groan, clutching her to him like she might slide out of his grasp in a stormy ocean.

It was some time—minutes maybe—before she recovered herself enough to have a semicoherent thought. She realized that her macaw was screaming blue murder. Also a phone was ringing in the living room. "Do shut up, Pepe!" Her voice was breathless, cracking.

"A witness," said Rigo, casting a doubtful glance at the bird. "Will we have to bribe him?"

Bella laughed. "That won't help. He'll scream your business to anyone if they have a few pistachio nuts."

"I suppose that would serve me right." Rigo's hair was tousled, a few strands stuck to his hot forehead, and his eyes dark with passion. "I didn't come over here to seduce you."

"Why did you come here? To give me a tardy notice?" She couldn't help teasing.

"To help you pack."

"You could have sent a staff member."

"True." He looked thoughtful. The phone started ringing again.

"That's not my phone," she murmured. She didn't want him to get up. She had a feeling that everything would change the moment their bodies peeled apart and the fog of shared passion lifted.

"It's mine." He groaned. "I suppose I should see who it is."

He eased off her carefully, stopping for a leisurely kiss on the way, then padded into the living room naked and barefoot. Bella stared after him from the bed, still in shock and unable to imagine lifting her head from the pillow.

"Perfect." She could hear Rigo's voice loud and clear from the other room.

He appeared in the doorway a moment later, tugging on his clothes. "I'm going to visit Francine Petrie the day after tomorrow."

His father's mistress.

He zipped up his jeans. "I have a feeling that she's a key to the murders."

Bella felt herself shrink back into the bedding. What did this woman know? Would the mysterious Francine be the key to putting her father behind bars?

"Don't worry about coming into work. I know you need to pack."

"I—" She couldn't move into his house and she needed to tell him but how? She'd better get somewhere else lined up first. She could spend the afternoon making phone calls.

She could hardly foist herself and all of her animals on a friend. Her single friends all had big jobs in London or Zurich or Paris. Her married friends had children and husbands to worry about.

Maybe she could find an empty farm cottage that needed renovation and do work on it in exchange for living there. She could set up an online fundraiser to raise money to feed the animals and pay their vet bills. An Internet marketer she'd met in New York had encouraged her to do that and to contact him with help making it effective.

"Thanks. I'll be in tomorrow, I promise." For now she wanted to keep her paycheck coming. All things considered it was a pretty good one. "And I won't tell anyone about...what happened."

Rigo shoved a hand through his hair. "That probably is the best policy." He looked distracted. She was pretty sure he hadn't turned up here for revenge sex. He was too thoughtful a lover—and a human—for that. Maybe he'd come here to see what she—or her father—was up to. Luckily, he was leaving none the wiser.

Rigo frowned. "This...morning's events have

nothing to do with your moving into my house. That comes with no obligation."

How sweet of him to say that! His words made the impossibility of the situation more agonizing. She had to let him know she wouldn't be moving. "Actually I've made other arrangements."

"Really?"

"Yes, a friend of my father's has a little house. It'll be perfect."

Rigo's eyes narrowed slightly. "Where is it?"

"Uh…" She racked her mind for Altaleone geography. "Over the hill behind…the old Kroll dairy."

A brow lifted. "Where the cement works is?"

"Uh." Whoops. "Not exactly. But in that general direction."

He stared at her for a moment, then turned and left without another word.

Bella stared at the door after it closed behind him. Why was she such a screwup? This whole adulting thing was exhausting.

Ari sauntered across the floor and laid himself in her lap. She stroked his soft head. "Thank goodness for all of you. You're what keeps me sane. And I'll figure it all out, I promise."

The next day she was dressing for work when another knock on the door startled her. Her heart pounded as she imagined Rigo standing there, but she opened the door to see Emma and Serena. "Hi!" Their in-unison greeting unnerved her. "We're walking around Casteleone today shooting a vlog for Serena's channel. We need you to help because you're actually from Altaleone and will give us authenticity."

Bella wanted to laugh. "Wouldn't Beatriz be better?"

"Beatriz is busy with her fashion line. We need you," said Emma decisively. "And that outfit is too boring." She gestured at Bella's unusually restrained dark gray ensemble. "Put on something more…you. You know, lace and ruffles and unnecessary belts."

Now Bella did laugh. "Thanks for summing up my style so succinctly. I guess this look is a bit of a downer." If only she could tell them what was going on with Rigo.

If only she had any idea what actually was going on with Rigo!

She wondered if they knew anything. She had kissed him in public at the wedding, after all.

"So, you and Rigo." Serena walked boldly into her apartment, to a volley of barking. "What's the scoop?"

Well, that answered one question, anyway.

"I really have no idea." She smiled and tried to look cool. "But I do know that I should behave with more professionalism where he's concerned and I intend to do so from now on." Phew. She hadn't admitted to anything specific, but that could encompass the kiss if they'd noticed it.

"Nonsense. Rigo is far too professional and needs to be dragged kicking and screaming into having a personal life." Emma bent down to pet Martini, who wound through her legs.

Not with someone whose father might have murdered his father. The thought flashed through her mind, chilling the faint spark of enthusiasm she felt at

Emma's warm words.

"Go on, get dressed," urged Serena, who had picked up Sapphire the rat and was stroking her gently. "We need to get cracking. We're going to go live on the hour, and we need to get in position for the first one in fifteen minutes."

"Can I bring Squiggles?"

"It wouldn't be a party without him."

The day flashed by in a whirlwind of visits to rustic cafés and ancient bakeries. They drove out to a prehistoric stone circle on a windswept hilltop and live-vlogged in a sudden shower of rain. Bella and Squiggles were exhausted by the time they finally headed back to the palace barely half an hour before dark.

"I really need to get home and feed my animals," she protested, not for the first time.

Emma and Serena shot each other what looked like a conspiratorial glance. "Okay, we'll drive you," said Serena.

"It's barely a ten-minute walk. I'll be fine."

"Actually it's kind of a long walk. At least an hour."

"More like two," chimed in Emma.

"What?"

"While we've been dragging you from pillar to post, movers have shifted all of your things and your animals into the old hunting lodge."

"What?" Panic clutched her chest.

Emma smiled. "Don't get mad at Rigo. It was our idea as much as his. And we hired a professional animal behaviorist to help keep it as stress-free as possible for all your animals."

Bella stared. She couldn't imagine that Pepe had taken kindly to being carted across Casteleone. There must have been a lot of screaming and plucking of feathers. "I can't believe you would do this without asking me." She felt...betrayed.

"We could tell that you were feeling weird about it, that you didn't want to be a burden, and that the move was going to be difficult with all your animals, so we took the bold and rather obnoxious step of taking it out of your hands." Serena looked apologetic. "I hope you'll forgive us eventually."

Bella felt tears spring to her eyes. Her anger evaporated into sadness as she realized they'd done it out of sheer kindness. Emma and Serena had no idea of the awkward position they'd put her in— living in the house of a man she'd had sex with— and who wanted to arrest her father for murder.

"All of my animals are there?" Her voice was a rasping whisper.

"Yes. And I've been getting texts from Mario— the animal trainer—that they're all doing fine. He's set up Pepe's cage by a shaded window, but you can move it wherever you want."

"Where's my car?"

"At the house. We had them move it so we could take you straight there."

"I feel like I've been swept away on a magic carpet." She tried to sound cheerful when she felt like she'd just had the rug pulled out from under her.

"Great! That's what we wanted." Emma hugged her. "Let's go."

Lights shone in the windows of the baronial

mansion as they drove up the long, straight drive. The building was as grand and gloomy as ever, and seemed like an impossible place for her to live.

Anxiety over her animals trumped her nerves at the awkward situation, and by the time they reached the front door her hurried entrance could probably be mistaken for enthusiasm. Suki and Tintin rushed at her as she walked in, and she knelt and hugged them tight. As least they were fine. Sure, they'd have to move again, but they'd have had to do that anyway. As long as she kept her focus on the animals, everything would work out eventually.

Wouldn't it?

"Would you like to look around?" Emma's eager expression suggested that she wanted to look around herself. They'd been so busy keeping her occupied all day they hadn't had time to explore the place.

"Sure." Her voice sounded flat. She hoped they weren't too excited about her living here and wouldn't take it personally when she ditched at the earliest opportunity. "Does Rigo really know I'm here?"

She wouldn't put it past them to move all her stuff in, then surprise him with the news.

"Oh, yes. He gave very specific instructions about the animals. He's having the old greenhouse screened so it can be an aviary for Pepe."

"What?"

"Yes. They're still wiring the lights out there because the house didn't have any outdoor lights."

Emotion welled in Bella's chest. How sweet of him. She didn't deserve this kind of treatment at all—but Pepe did and maybe that was who Rigo had focused on. "Where is Rigo?"

She didn't want to be surprised by him. She wasn't at all sure how she'd handle it. She was just as likely to break down sobbing as to thank him graciously.

"He's holed up with Gibran at the palace. Darias and Sandro are with them."

A cool knife of anxiety plunged into her belly. Had they found evidence against her father? "Oh. Okay. Let's look around." She tried to sound enthusiastic but failed miserably.

Still carrying Squiggles in his bag and with Tintin and Suki hot on her heels, she trailed around the ground-floor rooms, oohing and aahing at how bright the vast kitchen looked—they'd filled the fridge with goodies for her and the animals—and admiring the set of unused dinnerware, probably worth a small fortune, they'd retrieved from storage for her to use. She could picture her cats licking tuna off eighteenth-century Limoges porcelain.

Upstairs they visited Pepe, who seemed remarkably relaxed in his new surroundings—a grand bedroom with highly detailed plasterwork—preening his feathers rather than plucking them. He greeted her with a loud squawk, as if to say, "Finally, quarters worthy of my magnificence!"

Serena and Emma were clearly thrilled with all the work the movers had done. They'd even put her sheets on the grandest bed and her towels in the adjoining vintage bathroom. Bella felt like someone had gone through her underwear drawer—which they had.

When they finally left she was so relieved she wanted to sob, but she didn't want to scare the animals so she gritted her teeth and hummed a tune while she put their dinners together and topped up their water. The house was so large that her dogs and cats found endless amusement in climbing the stairs and sneaking around behind marble columns.

I need to phone Rigo to thank him. It was only polite. He—or the staff, anyway—had gone to a lot of trouble. But why should she thank him when she didn't want to be here at all?

She wanted to gnash her teeth and throw something with frustration at the impossible situation. Rigo was so kind and thoughtful—but also so principled and loyal to his own family and nation. Of course he wanted to find out who killed his father and grandmother—who wouldn't? If he thought her father was guilty of something of course he had to investigate. Even she was starting to have her doubts about him, though she still didn't believe he'd be involved in a murder.

Why Rigo he have to be so upstanding, so unassailable, so damn perfect? Worse yet, their attraction was mutual and they had amazing sex! She'd never met anyone like him, and she never would again.

Her distracted reverie was interrupted by someone banging on the door downstairs. They might have been knocking for a while She'd been so preoccupied with the animals she'd tuned out the outside world. More than a little wary about opening the door to this remote house in the dead of night, she crept down the stairs to see who it could be.

18

"Who is it?" The tall front door was solid, with no peephole. No doubt in the old days a butler had risked their life to open the door to unexpected visitors.

"It's me."

Rigo. Her heart rose and sank at the same time. First he'd moved her into his house lock, stock, and barrel like an errant concubine. Now he felt he could show up whenever he wanted.

And she couldn't wait to open the door and see him. She must be going insane.

She struggled with the long iron bolts at the top and bottom of the door—she and Emma and Serena had come in through a side door—and was almost breaking a sweat by the time she finally pulled the heavy door back on its creaking hinges.

The light from behind her illuminated his bold features and revealed an expression of eager curiosity that tugged at her insides. "Are all your animals settled in okay?"

"I can't believe you did this without telling me."

"I had a feeling you weren't going to move in."

She frowned. "Then why did you do it for me?"

"Because I realized I'd made things awkward by

sleeping with you and I didn't want you to feel like you had to move somewhere else."

"So without telling me you had all my animals carted over here."

"Exactly." His expression was changing to a more familiar one of arrogant superiority. Which was a relief. Now she could feel pique and annoyance rather than a disturbing tenderness for him.

"I hope I'm not expected to behave like some sort of...kept mistress." She lifted a brow. "I bet this was what your ancestors did with women they wanted to have sex with. Hole them up in a nice house so they'd never want to leave."

Rigo sighed. "There's no denying it is an awkward situation."

"The more so because you suspect my father of committing crimes against your family and the state."

His expression darkened. "Are you going to invite me in?"

"Is that one of the terms of my tenancy?" She was still angry enough to challenge him.

"I don't believe there are any terms to your tenancy since I haven't offered an agreement and you haven't signed one."

"So I'm here at your mercy."

"Pretty much." Exasperation with a hint of amusement sparkled in his eyes.

"Well then I guess you'd better come in." She put her hands on her hips and stepped aside. "Your majesty."

"Watch your tone, young lady." He swept past her. "Have you forgotten that I'm your boss?"

"Not for a single second."

Squiggles surprised her by racing across the polished wood floor and assailing Rigo, who picked him up and perched him on his arm.

"I can't believe he's not biting you."

"Squiggles is clearly a fine judge of character."

"Or a huge suck-up."

"He doesn't want to bite the hand that is currently feeding the hand that feeds him."

"I need to find another job," she challenged.

"Not really. Didn't your dad just give you a large cash sum?"

I'm not taking it. She wanted to throw the words at him, but that might imply that her dad was guilty.

"That money was supposed to buy my animal sanctuary building."

"Was?"

"My dad says it's coming. I'm not even sure he has it."

"Hmm, maybe he's not comfortable moving money around in his usual way when he knows that the security forces of Altaleone are watching all his movements."

Bella stared at him. "Did you come here to accuse my dad or to have sex with me? Neither seems appropriate, or anything but downright obnoxious under the circumstances."

Rigo had the decency to look contrite. "I'm sorry. I've been told that my brutal bluntness is one of my least attractive features."

"Though being an honest lawyer does make you original, at least." She lifted a brow. "And since I know I can count on your honesty, what have you learned? Is there some new break in the murder case?"

"I'm going to see Francine Petrie tomorrow. I hope she'll be the big break we're looking for."

"How?"

"She was my father's mistress and thus privy to a lot of his secrets and intimate thoughts. She might have some insight into the forces acting against him, if not the actual murderer."

"What makes you so sure she didn't murder him?"

Rigo hesitated a moment. "Maybe she did."

"You should watch your step when you go see her."

"You can watch my step for me. You're coming with me."

"Where does she live?"

"Liechtenstein. She's from there originally and we tracked her to her grandparents' farm, where she's living under her maiden name."

"What if she starts shooting at us?"

"We'll have security following us."

"Why is that not at all reassuring?"

"Are you afraid? You don't have to come."

Bella bristled. "I'm not afraid. And I'm pretty damn curious about this Francine. I'm coming."

"Excellent." An annoying satisfied smile spread across Rigo's face. Suddenly she wasn't sure if she wanted to slap or kiss it off him.

He decided for her by stepping forward and sweeping her into his arms for a powerful kiss that made her breath hitch. Her whole body sizzled with arousal by the time he finally let her up for air.

"What would your colleagues in New York say

about the way you shamelessly harass your assistant?"

"Who says I'm shameless?" he teased. "I'm racked with guilt right now." The twinkle of mischief in his eyes belied his comment.

"Then let's head upstairs and give you more to be guilty about." She took his hand and guided him toward the carved wood staircase that wound through the center of his own baronial mansion. It had been a long day, but the prospect of luring Rigo under the sheets of her strange bed was too tempting.

They kissed going up the stairs, groped each other in the upstairs hallway and soon reveled in each other's naked bodies in the dim half-light of the grand bedroom. Bella kissed him with frenzied passion that came with an edge of panic.

Tomorrow, Francine might point the finger at her father—and possibly other members of the creepy Cross of Blood society—and her world would crumble. Rigo's suspicions would be confirmed, her father would be arrested, and she'd become a pariah.

Until then she could live suspended in this magical half-world where she and Rigo came together, somewhere between royalty and responsibility, between common sense and madness. It couldn't last, but it was too wonderful while it did.

The next morning, Bella got the animals ready with water and made sure everyone who needed to go out had gone out, then she tucked Squiggles into Sapphire's favorite plush cat house, because there was no way she wanted to bring him along on what might turn out to be a dangerous misadventure. They set out early for Liechtenstein. The tiny country wasn't far away, but the roads were winding and mountainous so the drive to the remote farmstead took much of the morning.

A dark SUV with three security guards followed behind them at a distance and was often lost from view. Fields of cows and sheep, punctuated by remote mountain chalets, stretched on until at last Rigo muttered, "This is it."

They opened a gate leading into a field, and she closed it behind them while Rigo told the security staff to wait outside it. Bella felt her heart beat faster as they approached the small stone farmhouse, with its steep pitched roof. One old van with faded pale blue paint stood in the driveway. It certainly didn't look like the residence of a royal mistress.

They climbed out of the car and approached the green-painted door. Rigo knocked with impressive royal confidence, while Bella gritted her teeth and hoped they weren't about to face both barrels of a farmer's shotgun.

A petite woman with bright green eyes opened the door, and her hand flew to her reddish hair at the sight of Rigo. "It's been a long time."

If this was Francine she was quite a bit younger than Bella had imagined, and she reacted to Rigo almost as if he was the one she'd had the affair with, rather than his father. The mysterious Other Woman wore black-and-white-checked pencil pants and a fitted sweater that showed off her neat figure. Bella watched with growing curiosity as

Rigo coolly asked if they could come in.

Francine glanced doubtfully behind her, then glanced down the drive behind Rigo. "Who's in that black car?"

"Palace security. They're here to protect us. All of us, including you. I know you're scared, and that's why you're hiding here."

"Okay." Her pretty face looked pale and tense. "Come in."

Inside the cottage was less grim, painted a sunny yellow and decorated with pretty antiques and a collection of rooster-themed items. Francine must have noticed Bella staring because she said, "In feng shui roosters protect you from being gossiped about. I figured I needed as many as I could get."

Bella smiled. She really didn't know what was going on here. Why did she and Rigo know each other?

Francine seated them on a too-soft sofa, then sat in a chair opposite and lifted her chin. "I suppose you're going to ask if I murdered your father."

"Actually I was going to work backward toward that question," said Rigo drily. "I know you weren't investigated because no one—including my mother—knew of your existence."

"Except you."

"And I valued my mother's happiness too much to tell anyone about you."

"I saw in the papers that she just married again."

"Yes, and I hope she experiences the happiness you cheated her of."

"Your father wouldn't have been susceptible to

my charms if he was fully satisfied."

Rigo snorted. "You told me you were going to seduce him because I didn't want you."

"I admit I didn't realize it would turn into something. I did want the satisfaction of having one Leone man admire me."

Bella blinked. She felt like an intruder, yet they both seemed to have forgotten she was there.

"And it turned into a multiyear affair. Though I suppose the main attraction was the house he rented for you and all the expensive gifts he gave you."

"How did you know about those?"

"The numbers. It was all skillfully hidden, but I have a talent for forensic accounting. What I can't figure out is why you would kill your cash cow."

"I wouldn't." She shrugged and looked rueful. "My whole income flow ran dry the moment he was murdered. I left town because I was afraid someone would come after me because they thought I knew too much. I've been selling off his gifts and hiding away here for the last year since your brother Darias became king."

"Do you know who did it?"

"I have my suspicions. I warned your father in a letter."

Rigo's brows lowered. "I found it in his desk drawer. You didn't sign it, but it was pretty obviously from someone he was…intimate with. No one knew who it was from until I arrived."

"I'm flattered that you remembered me."

"Don't be." He frowned. "In the letter you tell him to beware the Cross of Blood. Why?"

"He told me his mother—the queen—wanted

to disband the society. She said she was too old for the kind of out-there sexual practices they were supposedly founded to provide, and that she thought their financial activities were outdated and elitist. She wanted the ancient funds to go to the people."

Bella glanced at Rigo, whose eyes narrowed. "And how did my father feel about this?"

"You know your father well enough to know that unless you could shoot it or eat it, he wasn't all that interested in it. And I can tell you firsthand that his sexual tastes were plain vanilla."

Rigo's expression didn't waver. "The finances. What do you know about them?"

"No more than you do, I'm sure. I don't think your father was privy to the details either, shocking as that is. I always thought that the remaining members seemed to have a lot of funds at their disposal, and I wondered if there was a fund they all dipped into."

Now Rigo glanced at Bella. "Bella and I have been looking for evidence of the same thing. I haven't been able to subpoena the Cross of Blood accounts because they're held in Switzerland. Darias followed royal tradition and joined the society, but they've kept him in the dark."

"I wrote the letter because I didn't think he saw the threat from them. It was too easy for him to ignore my fears when I said something so I wanted to put it on paper. He felt invincible— untouchable—as a royal, but I know enough about some of those men to know they're dangerous. Tears sprang to her bright eyes. "I loved Emil. I really did. I know he would never have left

Carolina for me, but he meant the world to me. I want you to catch his killers."

A muscle twitched in Rigo's jaw. "Do you have any idea which members are responsible, or are they all in it together?"

"I never met any of them, but I did overhear a heated conversation with someone he called Maurice or Bernice or something."

Bella's blood chilled. Her father.

She felt Rigo's eyes dart toward her, and she steeled herself not to show any emotion. "What were they talking about?" she asked as calmly as she could manage.

"Emil was saying that nothing stays the same forever, that even traditions need to change with the times. He said something about having a free ride since the Crusades and how it was time to put the people of Altaleone first." She pushed a tear away from her eye. "It was his mother's idea to change things, and he went along with her. I warned him they might be dangerous. Money can make people do crazy things."

"I intend to bring the murderers to justice. I will need you to testify about my father's intentions, since none of the rest of us was privy to his and my grandmother's plans for the Cross of Blood funds. So far we haven't had enough solid evidence to subpoena the members' individual financial records. All we have is their tax returns, which are suggestive but don't prove anything."

Her eyes grew wide. "I can't. They'll kill me. I don't dare show my face in Altaleone. They don't know how little I really know."

"Palace security will protect you."

"The way they protected Emma from getting kidnapped and Sandro from getting shot?"

Rigo frowned. "My father would have wanted you to help capture his killer."

Another tear rolled down her cheek. "I know. I was so angry when I heard the rumors of how they were found. Your father was never into...any of that S&M stuff."

Rigo's eyes flashed with suspicion. "How did you hear about the circumstances of the murders? That information was never released."

Was Francine herself involved in the murders? Bella's gut tightened. The security staff at the end of the driveway couldn't do a whole lot for them if she suddenly pulled a gun.

19

Francine's laugh chilled Bella's blood. "You think I was involved?"

"How else would you know about the kink angle?"

Francine waved a manicured hand. "You know how word gets around. Probably leaks from the palace staff. Wasn't one of them later found to be an enemy? At least the salacious details didn't find their way into the press." She hesitated and picked a piece of fluff from her sleeve. "Yet."

"Is that a threat?" Rigo's brow lifted.

"Not even slightly. Until you find that killer, my life is in danger. They know I was your father's confidante. He talked about the trouble he was having with the secret society. His mother was growing older and wanted to set things right before she died. She said that they should expose the society's doings to the people of Altaleone if they didn't agree to disband the society and give the funds to the public. Your father was just trying to implement her wishes."

"I need you to repeat this to the police."

Francine swallowed, clearly nervous. "I'm scared, I can't deny it, but I'll do it."

Darias nodded slowly. "I'll be in touch again soon. And I'm going to leave a security detail here to protect you. I intend to blow the lid off this conspiracy and see what's left when the dust settles.

Bella's gut churned as they walked back to the car. Francine Petrie had mentioned her father by name. Rigo didn't speak. He seemed deep in thought.

He gave the guards instructions to stay and guard the farmhouse and said he was heading back to Altaleone immediately.

Once they climbed into the car and closed the doors, he started the engine. "I want you to call the television station. Tell them I have an announcement about the murders and I'd like to be on air as soon as possible."

Bella pulled out her phone, pulse thudding. "Who should I call? Do you have a contact there?" She couldn't stop her voice from shaking.

"Ask for the news producer." He pulled out onto the road, his face taut.

Are you going to accuse my father? The words hovered on her lips as she searched for the station number and dialed it. With Rigo's name it didn't take more than a minute before she was talking to the news producer and calculating how long it would take them to drive to the station in Casteleone.

"What are you going to say?" She tried to sound calm, like she didn't really care either way.

"Since we have no way of knowing for sure if this car is bugged, I'm going to reserve my words for the television studio."

"Oh. Okay." His words chilled her. Did he no longer trust her? Maybe he'd never trusted her. Maybe all along he'd been playing her, trying to extract information about her father. He'd drawn her closer, pulling her into his arms, into his house, into his bed—all so he'd be perfectly positioned to point the finger at her dad.

Rigo was uncomfortably silent on the drive. She could almost hear his legal mind whirring. Luckily, she wasn't foolish enough to expect sweet nothings from Rigo at the best of times, but she wondered what he intended to do with her once he'd made his accusations.

Did he maybe even see her as some kind of accessory after the fact? He knew her father had arranged to pay her to kiss him in public.

Her nerves were getting the best of her by the time they pulled into the TV station parking lot. "Do you want me to stay in the car?"

"No." He spoke gruffly, but she told herself it was because he was distracted and preoccupied. "Come with me."

"I won't have to go on TV, will I?" The idea terrified her. She'd never been good at thinking on her feet. What if she unwittingly said something that incriminated her dad? Or even herself?"

"No. I just want you in here out of harm's way."

The TV station was quite small, like the entire country, so there was only one studio and a magazine program was underway when they were ushered in. A glamorous familiar-looking blonde hostess was laughing over a fluff story with the chiseled male anchor when the producer spoke through their headsets to tell them "Prince Rigo is ready. In three, two, one…."

Immediately their faces grew solemn, and the female hostess announced that Prince Rigo had news about the murders. Bella hugged herself as Rigo marched out onto the set, squinting against the bright lights, and took a seat next to them.

Rigo explained that he'd been personally investigating the circumstances behind the murders and had determined that they were carried out by a member or members of the ancient society called Cross of Blood, which ostensibly existed to protect the monarchy, but actually functioned as a means of perpetuating tax-free wealth among an elite cadre of aristocrats. He said that some or possibly all of the members were likely involved in both murders, and that he wouldn't quit until all of the perpetrators were brought to justice.

He spoke with such force that Bella felt a thrill at the idea that justice would finally be served— until she remembered that her father was one of the accused. No wonder Rigo had a reputation for victory in the courtroom.

The hosts pressed for details, but Rigo simply said that arrests were imminent and he was confident all the details would come out during the trial process.

In less than ten minutes they were heading out the door again, Rigo's face as hard and grim as ever.

"Where to now?" She could barely speak.

"Back to the palace."

Relief at the promise of relative safety at the palace warred with the realization that she was still essentially a traitor in their midst. Her father had planted here there as an unwitting mole, and Rigo had turned her into a double agent.

She couldn't even "go home" as her home was now Rigo's house. "I should get back to my animals."

"It's not safe to go alone. Someone at the palace can drive you."

She felt increasingly trapped. Maybe that was the point. Rigo ignored her. He had other things on his mind.

She followed him out to the car feeling like a prisoner. He had her right where he wanted her—until he didn't want her.

They climbed into the car, and Rigo started the engine. Bella's emotions rose as they pulled out of the parking lot onto the village streets. What would happen to her now? Would she even be allowed to go see her animals or had someone already arranged for a team of hired experts to take care of them while she was dragged into police headquarters and forced to testify against her father.

"What's the matter?" asked Rigo.

She realized her breathing must be audible. "What's going to happen to my dad?"

"I suppose that depends on how well he cooperates with police." Rigo was cool as if he was talking about a stranger in a foreign country.

People always said you should never trust a lawyer. They were too skilled at playing the angles. She was just another angle. "You don't think of people's feelings at all, do you?" Tears welled in her eyes, blurring the town's ancient streets.

Suddenly the car window blew out and sprayed her with shattered glass. She screamed and turned to Rigo. "Are you okay?" Tiny pieces of glass bit into her skin.

The car kept going, but she realized Rigo wasn't driving. His hands fell from the wheel as the vehicle mounted a curb and rammed into a parked car. The airbag inflated in her face, blowing more glass fragments at her.

Panic shot through her as she saw Rigo slumped, lifeless, in the seat next to her.

"Help!" She wrestled with her seat belt. Had he been shot? She couldn't see any blood. She struggled to get out of the car. "Help!" Where was her phone? Already a crowd of strangers had started to gather. The alarm of the car they'd hit was wailing. "Call an ambulance! He's hurt."

She rushed around to Rigo's side in a panic and struggled with the door, still screaming for help. There was blood on her hands and arms and on Rigo's face.

"Don't move him!" called a man's deep voice. She wheeled around half expecting to meet an armed assailant, but it was a uniformed policeman. "Help is on the way."

"It's Prince Rigo," she pleaded, hoping his royal status would get him help faster.

The policeman reached into the car and took Rigo's pulse with his hand. He hesitated for a moment, listening.

"Is he alive?"

"What happened?"

"I don't know! He was driving and then the window exploded." It had all happened so fast, and the sound of the window breaking had blotted out anything else.

"I think it was a bullet," said someone in the crowd behind her. "From a gun with a silencer."

"Everyone take cover!" boomed the policeman. "There's an active shooter." He pulled out his radio and spoke some unintelligible code into it, then drew his gun and scanned the streets and buildings.

"Get down!"

Bella hesitated. She didn't want to leave the car and Rigo's side. "Is he breathing? Will he be okay?"

"If help gets here fast enough."

Police cars screeched into the intersection and more uniformed officers dove out into the street. Bella worried that there wouldn't be room for the ambulance to get through, but soon it arrived and Rigo was carefully loaded onto a board and bundled in—still not moving.

"Can I come too?"

"Who are you?" asked a gruff, strange policeman.

"I'm...I'm his assistant. I was in the car with him."

They grudgingly let her into the ambulance, and she watched with increasing panic as they took his vitals and started IVs and talked in confusing medical jargon.

"Will he be okay?"

"We don't know what's wrong with him," said a sympathetic woman at last. "There's no gunshot wound. He's not losing blood, but he's unconscious. We don't know what hit him or where."

One of them cleaned up her wounds, superficial

scratches from the glass that stung from the antiseptic. She was too stunned to cry, which was fine because crying wouldn't help.

At the hospital she was led into a painfully bright lobby waiting area and Rigo disappeared through some double doors. She realized she'd left her bag and her phone behind her so she couldn't even call the palace to tell them what happened.

She went up to the receptionist. "Is there a phone I can use?" But before she could answer the glass door flung open and Sandro and Darias charged in. "Where is he?"

"Inside," she stammered. "He might be in surgery. No one's told me anything." Finally the tears came and she cursed them. She needed to be strong for the family.

The brothers pushed out of the waiting area into the surgical hallway, royal privilege on their side. She hovered behind, not sure what to do. Rigo couldn't die, could he?

The thought filled her with horror. Her heart ached with the depth of her feelings for him. Feelings that had been quietly growing since their first encounter when he rescued her in a crowded airport.

And whoever shot at him was still out there. Emma burst in through the doors. "Oh, my goodness, Bella! You're so lucky you weren't shot."

"I didn't even hear a bullet." Her voice was shaking. "I don't know what happened. I feel so useless." She hugged Emma tight, grateful for the reassuring human contact.

"The police have apprehended the shooter. They stormed every building on the surrounding blocks, and he was caught escaping over a roof on Croix Street."

"Who was it?"

"I don't know yet. How's Rigo doing?"

"He was still unconscious when they brought him in, and I haven't heard any news. Darias and Sandro are back there. They didn't find a bullet wound. What if he never wakes up? I'd just accused him of having no feelings."

She hoped the confession would give her a sense of relief, but it only twisted the knife in her gut.

"Let's go back there." Emma grabbed her hand and headed for the door to the surgical suites. No one tried to stop them, and they soon found Darias and Sandro talking to a doctor.

"You're not going to believe this." Darias's smile shocked Bella. "Rigo was knocked unconscious by his cell phone. He has a big knot on his forehead. They found the cell phone down behind his seat."

"Is he awake?" asked Bella, breathless.

"He's pretty dazed. The first thing he did was ask about you, though. Go in and see him."

Bella's heart swelled with joy. At least he hadn't died with her cold words wringing in his ears.

She opened the door gingerly. Rigo lay in bed in a hospital gown. A purple bruise darkened his temple. His gaze hit her with force as she entered. "You're wrong, you know." His voice was gruff.

Her heart sank. "About my father?" Did Rigo think her father had shot him? Panic flashed through her.

"About my feelings." His mouth hitched on one

side. "I thought I was too objective, too…logical to have feelings. I thought I'd pushed them aside along with procrastination and sleeping in and other enemies to my productivity."

His dark gaze rooted her to the spot. "But unfortunately I discovered I was wrong."

"How unfortunately?" Her heart filled with irrational hope.

"I find that I have feelings that are most inconvenient and unprofessional."

"How annoying." She battled a smile. Really he was being quite rude. Which meant he was being Rigo. Which made him oddly and infuriatingly irresistible to her…

His mouth tightened. "Naturally I would never allow my feelings to interfere with my royal duty."

Her belly tightened. "Of course." His feelings weren't going to stop him putting her father behind bars. Again, Rigo to the core.

"But I would never hold it against a certain young lady that she had divided loyalties. I quite understand how you can love someone even when they've committed acts you find reprehensible."

He watched her with those cool, dark eyes. Was he talking about his father's secret affair with Francine Petrie?

"He is my father."

"As my father was mine. It's in the nature of men to be greedy—for money, for women. It doesn't make them evil. I do think your father was involved in shady financial transactions, but I don't think he murdered my father and grandmother. And the murderer in South Africa just confessed to killing the accountant for his wallet and phone. He said that with his lawyer's help he picked your father's name off a list of company directors to try for a plea bargain. It was in alphabetical order so Beauvoir was first."

Relief fell over her like a rainstorm. "Really? So my father had nothing to do with it?"

"Nope."

Bella blinked. This was almost too good to be true. "But what about the murders here?"

"We still have to identify the true culprit, but I have a feeling that tonight's announcement will flush him out."

"Him?"

"I'm pretty sure I know who it is, but first I have something more important to address."

"What?" She stepped forward, wondering if he expected her to whip out her phone to take notes. It was probably still in the car. She realized with a chill that it was likely her phone that knocked him unconscious. He usually kept his in his back pocket, whereas she always put hers in the cup holder.

Rigo looked at her with a deadly serious expression—as if he was interrogating a witness. "Will you marry me?"

20

Bella stared at him. "You can't be serious."

"Have you ever known me to be anything else?"

"No, but you did just get a hard knock on the head."

His smile lines crinkled. "I assure you I am in full possession of my faculties."

She blinked. This didn't make sense. Of course she was crazy about him. He was brilliant, determined, passionate, principled, and damned sexy. But she was—

"I'm probably the worst assistant you've ever had. I bring a ferret to work."

"I adore you for bringing a ferret to work. It shows that you take your responsibilities to your animals seriously, that you have a caring heart, and that you're not afraid to stand up to authority."

She had to laugh. "I suppose that is true."

"And I swear I'm not just entranced by your beauty but by your whole character. You're kind and warm and get on well with everyone—utterly unlike myself."

"They do say that opposites attract."

"Indeed they do. And being a practiced judge of character I have a pretty good idea that you're attracted to me."

"Is it that obvious?"

"Maybe I flatter myself and you were just trying to seduce me to spare your father." The crinkled laugh lines in his face suggested he didn't believe it.

"Maybe I was." She lifted a brow, trying to look mysterious but couldn't suppress her smile. "Then again you probably have already figured out that I'm not that cagey."

"One of the many things I admire and adore about you. You're a straight shooter."

"With a taste for ruffles and lace."

"I enjoy your originality." He shifted on the pillows. "But you still haven't answered my question."

Anxiety spiked in her gut, warring with the joy that had surged through her at his unexpected compliments. "I'm not sure you've thought this through. You live in New York, and I need to open an animal sanctuary in Altaleone. There isn't a single sanctuary in the whole country."

He looked surprised. "You wouldn't move to New York for me?"

She bit her lip. "I tried New York, remember? It's too intense for me. And I think Squiggles would find the noise level stressful."

"True." He stared at her for a moment, dark eyes roaming over her face. "Then I'll have to move my practice to Altaleone. I know my brother Darias would appreciate the help, and some of our laws need to be rewritten. I could also do work for the United Nations and other international organizations based in Europe."

He seemed to be trying to convince himself—

which amazed her. "You'd really consider uprooting your whole life for me?"

He looked perplexed. "You don't seem to understand that I'm madly in love with you."

"I had no idea." Her mind spun. "I've been falling in love with you since the first time you scowled at me. I thought you found me exasperating and incompetent."

He looked stunned. "We've made love…"

"Some men will do that even with women they despise."

"Not me." He studied her intently. "As you well know I'm quite willing to kiss a total stranger, especially if she's a damsel in distress, but I draw the line at sleeping with them. I think you'd be surprised by how few women have shared my bed."

"Intriguing. May I join you?" She gestured at his narrow hospital bed.

"Please do." A wolfish grin spread across his mouth. She eased in next to him, enjoying the way her body seemed to come alive in his presence. She kissed his cheek very softly. "You're full of surprises."

"Not as many as you. I suppose no one expects me to have any surprises, like I'm a steel filing cabinet or something."

"You certainly are made of steel." She poked playfully at his hard chest. "Do you hurt anywhere?"

"Well…" He narrowed his eyes playfully. "I am becoming uncomfortably aroused."

"I don't think we can do anything about that until we get you out of here." Desire sizzled inside her. Making love to Rigo was the easiest thing in the world. She could do that all day and all night.

But marrying him? "So, if I marry you?" She assumed a very serious expression, like Rigo wore much of the time. "Do I become a princess?"

"Yes. I'm afraid you do."

"Hmm." She pretended to look thoughtful. "Is there a tiara involved?"

"You'd have to check with Emma and Serena, but I suspect there might be."

"What if it gets tangled in my hair?" She gestured at her long, loose curls that had exploded out of their bun some time between the gunshot and now.

"That's a risk you'd have to take."

She couldn't imagine their lives together. It was such a huge leap from all-powerful boss and clueless ferret-carrying admin to... "Wait a second. Is this why you had them move me into your house? Is that where we're going to live?"

"Where we're going to live. I like the sound of that. And you have to admit, it does make sense."

"My animals are probably wondering where I am. It must be getting close to dinner. I suspect they want to keep you here, but do you think they'll let me observe you myself instead of using all these annoying machines?" She gestured at the monitors hooked up to him."

"I'm going to take the risk of declaring myself fully recovered." He peeled off a sensor that was taped to his chest. "But we still have a problem. I'm finding you as evasive as some of my most prickly and difficult defendants. Are you ever going to answer my question?"

Bella bit her lip. Was it really possible? Could she marry Rigo and live happily ever after? The situation was fraught with pitfalls—neither of them knew what would happen with her father, and unlike Emma and Serena, who were effortlessly elegant and poised at all times, she wasn't really cut out to be a royal bride.

But could she ever be happy again if she didn't?

"Would it be okay if we had a long engagement so we can be sure we're not both crazy?"

He stared at her for a moment, then a smile creased his mouth. "I think that could be arranged."

"I'd be lying if I didn't say that I'm questioning your sanity right now, but you're a grown man—and a very intelligent one at that—so I'm going to give you the benefit of the doubt. Especially since I've also fallen madly in love with you."

"Thank God." She watched Rigo's chest heave, then he took her in his arms and enveloped her in a kiss so long and hard that she saw stars and started to wonder if maybe she'd been hit on the head as well.

When they finally parted he looked long and hard into her eyes. "I love you."

Her chest swelled with joy. "I'm still wondering if you're going to recover from this head injury and take it all back, but I really do love you, too." She realized they'd been left alone a long time. "Where's your family?"

"I told them to go home and give me some time alone with you." Mischief shone in his eyes.

"Once again you exhibit an alarming level of self-confidence."

"It's one of my best assets." He shot her a cheeky grin that heated her insides.

"You forgot one thing: Our car isn't drivable due to being filled with broken glass and other evidence."

"Not to worry. I had Darias arrange for another to be brought to the hospital."

"What if someone tries to shoot us on the way home?"

"This one has bulletproof glass so we'll continue on our merry way."

"How are you so cool and composed in every situation?"

"Royal blood." He winked.

They found the bulletproof SUV outside, being guarded by security staff, who also followed them home, one car driving in front of them and one behind them. Rigo spent much of the drive on the phone following the progress of the Altaleone police arresting all members of the Cross of Blood and some of their associates. Bella drove, wondering if she was going to wake up from this dream and laugh at herself for believing it.

The animals were beside themselves when they finally arrived home. They ran around Rigo and jumped up on him, the dogs barking and the cats purring and even Squiggles making his excited squeaky noise. She put Sapphire on her shoulder, then let Pepe out of his cage and let him flap around in the great hall downstairs. "I don't think they'll believe me if I tell them we get to live here for good."

"They'll discover it day by day as they settle in here and get used to it. And we can build some nice outdoor enclosures for them."

"I was oohing and aahing over the walled garden when I visited here before the wedding. That's the perfect place for them to roam. And there's plenty of room for more animals." She snuck a glance at Rigo. "Are you okay with my animal sanctuary being right here or do you want me to keep the animals somewhere else?"

He looked confused. "How would we take care of them if they're somewhere else? There are five hundred acres of pasture and woods. You could rescue every animal in Altaleone if you wanted."

She didn't know whether to laugh or cry. "It's too perfect. I'm not used to that."

"Don't worry, stuff will go wrong." He pulled her close and kissed her forehead. "And we'll figure out how to fix it together."

She rested her head against his chest and let her weight sink into him for a moment, while Sapphire climbed from her shoulder onto Rigo's. For the first time in...maybe her whole life, she felt like she could rely on someone for support. It still felt too good to be true, but she decided to go with it.

The next day at the palace, Rigo announced their engagement to the rest of the family, who seemed to have magically all gathered there for lunch. Rigo suspected the female Leones of anticipating the need for a party and silently admired their intuition. The women couldn't hide their excitement, and Darias, Sandro, and Lorenzo clapped Rigo on the back and congratulated him on joining the club.

After they'd toasted with champagne, Rigo had

to get down to business. "Darias, has Gibran questioned the Cross of Blood members?"

"Yes, and they're falling like dominoes. All of them admit to taking large payouts from an account that's disbursed tax-free profits for hundreds of years in secret. While none of them has directly accused anyone of the murder, they all fingered Artelgard Vernis as the mastermind behind their activities."

A thrill of satisfaction warmed him. Francine had thought she'd overheard his father talking about Maurice, but perhaps it was Vernis—the name sounded similar when pronounced in her accent. Vernis was from an ancient Altaleone family with several unprofitable vineyards and a lavish lifestyle. "What did Artelgard Vernis say?"

Sandro chimed in. "He said Darias had ordered the murder of his father and grandmother so he could be king."

Rigo stared. "You're kidding me."

Darias lifted a brow. "I think you all know me better than that."

"We do," said Rigo with a sigh. "So it looks like we have our man. Have you frozen the funds?"

"It's underway. And I intend for the funds to be transferred to Altaleone, where they will become part of the public trust and fund schools and roads and our future, rather than just lining the pockets of a few rich aristocrats for centuries."

"What's the plan for the Cross of Blood members?" Out of the corner of his eye Rigo could see Bella tensing.

"We'll have to determine which were involved in the murders, and they'll be prosecuted to the fullest extent of the law. For those involved only in the financial transactions, we're thinking a hefty amount of community service might be appropriate."

Rigo glanced at Bella and saw her eyes brighten. He couldn't quite imagine her father planting daffodils in the public square or picking up trash after the summer concerts, but it would certainly be better than prison.

"And the sniper who shot at us?"

"In custody. He's not talking but we're looking for the source of funds that entered his bank account yesterday. Signs point to Artelgard Vernis again."

"I want to talk to him?" Rigo wanted to question him.

"Good. I have a feeling that once you square off with him he'll tell us everything."

"That's my plan."

Lina pressed her hands together. "Do you think we'll really have peace again after so long?"

"Yes, Mama, I really believe we will," said Darias. "And the millions—possibly billions—stashed away in the secret account, will help ensure a bright future for everyone in Altaleone. Now all I have to do is convince Rigo to stay here to be our attorney general."

"Good luck with that," quipped Beatriz.

"Funny you should mention it," said Rigo, with a sly glance at Bella. "But Bella and I are planning to stay here so I find myself in need of a new job."

"You're moving back to Altaleone?" Lina's eyes widened.

"Bella has important work to do saving all the

animals in Europe. I couldn't interfere with that. And there's a lot of human rights work to do here."

"That there is," agreed Amadou. "I look forward to working with you on anti-trafficking prosecutions."

"While that seems a strange thing to look forward to, the feeling is mutual." A warm smile spread across his face. For the first time in years, Rigo felt like he was exactly where he was supposed to be. "I don't plan to spend all my time on the law anymore," he confessed. "I have some elaborate animal pens to construct."

Bella's lovely smile lit up his heart. "And golden eagles to observe."

"Bella's opened my eyes to a lot of things," he murmured. "And I know there'll be many more to come." He leaned in and kissed her on the lips in front of everyone—no rescue, reward, or revenge involved.

"You two are adorable," said Serena.

"I never thought I'd hear the word *adorable* in a sentence about Rigo," said Beatriz, shaking her head.

"It's a new era for the royal house of Leone," said Rigo with a wry grin. "Apparently anything is possible."

EPILOGUE

The following spring

"I don't mind the press at all." Bella glanced at the phalanx of photographers seated in their own special pavilion on the lawn. Her heart was so filled with joy today she could hug pretty much anyone. "It's great publicity for the animal shelter. Every time there's a story about us in the press money pours in."

"And animals," said Rigo with a grin. "We got a flock of eight heritage-breed sheep last week when media coverage leading up to the wedding started."

"Aren't they lovely?" Bella pointed to the sweet black-faced sheep where they grazed on a wide area of lawn not far from the wedding guests. "And they're eco-friendly mowing, too."

"Your dress is stunning." Her cousin Ani kissed her cheek.

"Thanks, my new sister-in-law Beatriz designed it." It had big, bold sleeves, a tiny waist, and acres of skirt covered in incredible embroidery detail.

"And so is that necklace," said Beatriz.

Bella fingered the dramatic diamond-and-sapphire flowers at her collar bone. "It was found among our dad's things at the Orangerie. Darias contacted the jeweler and discovered that he'd had it made for his mother's birthday, but they were both killed before he could give it to her."

"And we decided that only one other person in the family could pull it off," said Emma with a smile.

Darias slipped his arm around his wife's waist. "Grandma would have loved you, Bella. And so would my dad."

"I'm sorry I never knew them, but I'm glad their killer has been brought to justice." Artelgard Vernis and several hired hit men had been sentenced to life, and a number of conspirators were serving shorter sentences. Mercifully, her father wasn't among them.

"Your whole look is so...you," said Serena with a smile. Sandro stood next to her, holding their eight-month-old son Alessioin his arms.

"I know." Bella laughed. "A little eccentric—"

"And a lot fabulous," said Lina. "You're a miracle worker. I can't believe the transformation you've worked in Rigo. Before you we could barely get him on the phone, and now we see him all the time."

"And he's always smiling." Beatriz shook her head. "I barely recognize him."

"Look who's talking," said Sandro. "You've transformed from being a quiet bookworm who rarely left the palace grounds to the talk of Milan, and your smile is bigger than Rigo's."

Beatriz gave her husband, Lorenzo, a loving look. "It just shows what can happen when you meet the right person to help you finally break out

of your shell. Before I met Lorenzo the biggest
decisions of the day were whether to ride hunter or
dressage that morning and which book to read in
the afternoon. This morning I learned that
Printemps, one of the biggest department stores in
Paris, is opening a boutique with my name on it."

"Sandro helped me out of my shell, too," said
Serena with a smile. "I was all alone, hiding from
the world and licking my wounds when Sandro
blasted into my life and changed everything."

"And Serena made me realize I was ready to
settle down and have a family." He smiled
indulgently at his tiny son.

"Baa!" cried Alessio, clapping his chubby hands
together, a big, drooly smile on his face. "Baa baa!"

"I was teaching him animal noises this
morning," admitted Bella. "Starting with our new
sheep."

"Gee, thanks, sis," said Sandro with a wink.
"We'll be sure to share live video when he does it
at three a.m."

"You're welcome." Bella grinned. How was it
possible that these privileged royals were so warm
and welcoming? For the first time in her life she
felt like she was part of a real family. Even her
father was being nicer to her, calling more often
and accepting her invitations to lunch and dinner
whenever she asked him. Her becoming a princess
probably had something to do with it, but she'd
take his attention however she could get it.

The wedding planner hurried over, "It's time!"

Bella drew in a deep breath. All the guests were
seated on the lawn. Between the rows of seats, a
wide aisle of grass led toward a pretty pavilion that

the florist had magically covered with live vining roses. A small flock of rescued geese pecked at the grass behind it, and two of her newest friends, both shelter volunteers, stood nearby, keeping Pepe, Sapphire, and the gang in check so they could watch the ceremony, too.

Rigo had been hanging back, pressured by the traditionalists to stay away from her until the ceremony, and she caught her first glimpse of him as he walked toward the pavilion.

Bella's father ahemed quietly, and she slipped her arm into his. As they walked up the aisle she allowed herself to feast on the vision of Rigo, tall, regal, implacable, a pillar of truth and justice…and all hers. She wouldn't have believed it possible for her to love anyone this much—at least not anyone with only two legs. And to think she had to thank a long string of misfortunes—beginning with her unwitting liaison with a married man and her father being suspected of murder—for her incredible luck in getting to know him.

As she and her father walked up the aisle, her skirt so voluminous that he risked tripping on it as much as she did, she said a quick prayer of thanks that her father had only been found guilty of being a greedy aristocrat attempting to live by ancient laws in the modern world. The Cross of Blood was now officially disbanded, and its deep coffers opened to benefit the people of Altaleone, not just a small cadre of blue bloods.

Her father let go of her hand as she reached Rigo, and she felt a huge goofy smile spread across her face. As usual Rigo's hard features resembled the nearby mountains, but now his eyes twinkled with familiar joy that warmed her heart.

"I love you," he whispered as she drew close.

"I love you, too."

A smile tugged at his mouth while the officiant cleared his throat as if to scold them for talking out of turn. As the officiant rambled on in their native tongue, she let her mind wander to all the things she and Rigo had planned, including children of their own one day. Serena's adorable baby had lit a fuse of baby fever throughout the family, and Emma was already pregnant with a tiny royal heir.

"Do you, Rigoberto Montefiore Andante Charlemagne Leone take Arabella Ysatis Mirabelle Beauvoir to be your bride, to love and cherish her as long as you both shall live?"

The sound of their pompous full names almost made her giggle, but she managed to suppress it as Rigo said, "I do," in his deep, sonorous voice.

"And do you, Arabella Ysatis—"

"I do!" she burst out, unable to contain herself. "I absolutely do."

A murmur of laughter spread through the crowd, and she felt it rumble in her chest.

"I now pronounce you man and wife." The ancient and dignified priest looked sternly at Rigo. "You may kiss the bride."

Rigo, still deadly serious, gathered her in his arms and kissed her so hard and long that she almost forgot where they were. The moment they pulled apart, the audience erupted in applause. She wondered if that was normal during a wedding, but then who really cared what was normal or what wasn't? Her father beamed—as well he might, since he'd played a huge role in bringing her together with her handsome prince. Even if he'd done it for the wrong reasons, everything had worked out for all the right ones.

People started laughing and pointing and after a moment of alarm she realized that during the ceremony the sheep had wandered over to the pavilion and were now nibbling on the spectacular climbing roses. "Hey, you're sheep, not goats, stop that!"

Rigo laughed. "Let them feast, and we'll go enjoy our feast. This way!" And he led them back down the aisle toward the walled garden, where a huge banquet was laid out—with special treats for each of the animals—and they ate and sang and danced late into the night.

THE END

The complete Royal House of Leone Series:

The King's Bought Bride (Darias and Emma)
A Prince for Christmas (Sandro and Serena)
The Prince's Secret Baby (Sandro and Serena)
The Princess and the Player (Lina and Amadou)
The Princess's Scandalous Affair (Beatriz and Lorenzo)
Taming the Royal Beast (Rigo and Bella)

For more information visit www.jenlewis.com.

ABOUT THE AUTHOR

Jennifer Lewis loves heat in all its forms including spicy food, steamy temperatures and smoking hot heroes. She is a USA TODAY bestselling author and her books have been translated into more than twenty languages. She lives in sunny South Florida and when she's not sitting at her laptop she can often be found at the beach. Read more about her books and join her new release mailing list at www.jenlewis.com.